Hero Unmasked

Anna Alexander

Hero Unmasked
Anna Alexander
Book three in the Heroes of Saturn series.

When Dhavin Kilsgaard landed on Earth, he knew trading his life as a royal guard for a position as a small-town police officer would take some adjusting. But not even his skills at foiling assassination attempts and protecting princesses prepared him for the complexity that is the human female. Fiona Corrione's shy smile makes him hunger for more than a taste of the delicious chocolate she sells in her candy store, but the woman won't fall for his Llanos charm.

When his empathetic abilities sense her lusty cravings for his superhero alter ego, he doesn't hesitate to seduce her from behind the mask. Once she falls in love with him, she'll forgive him for the ruse, right?

Fiona is beyond livid when she discovers the flirtatious officer and her hunky hero lover are one and the same. Before she kicks Dhavin to the curb, she'll prove Earth girls aren't easy and revenge is sweetest when served with leather straps and whipped cream.

Dedication

For my family. Always.

Acknowledgement

You never know when inspiration will strike or when the answers to your plotting obstacles will be answered. When fellow author Eilis Flynn invited me to present a workshop with her at Geek Girl Con in Seattle, I didn't know the core of Dhavin's story would find me there. The purpose of the Con is to inspire and celebrate the role of women in predominately male-oriented venues such as science, art and education, and it was here where the idea of Dhavin having to explore the challenges of having a dual identity was born. Thank you, Eilis for the opportunity and thanks to Geek Girl Con for offering a platform for women to stand proud doing what they love.

Find Anna Online

Website

annaalexander.net

Facebook

facebook.com/pages/Anna-Alexander/282170065189471

Twitter

twitter.com/AnnaWriter

Newsletter

http://eepurl.com/Q0tsz

Chapter One

"**H**E'S HERE! HE'S here!" Margery squealed as she dashed into the kitchen, nearly upsetting the tray of cookies in Fiona's arms.

"Watch it, Mags," she shouted and steadied the tray of black-and-whites. "Who's here?"

A deep, testosterone-filled rumble followed by a chorus of tittering laughter peeled from the front of the store, cluing her in as to who was the cause of Mags' excitement.

Fiona blew at the strands of hair stuck in her lashes, determined to ignore the teeny-tiny tingle of excitement fluttering under her ribs. "Oh. Him."

"Yes, *him*." Mags sighed and slicked on a layer of pink lip gloss. Tossing the tube into her purse, she then reworked her long, blonde ponytail. "Haven't you noticed he comes in every Tuesday and Friday morning? It's my favorite times of the week."

Of course Fiona noticed that the too-too handsome Officer Dhavin Kilsgaard frequented her little shop a few times a week, she just hadn't recorded his visits to memory. His routine was one of the many things about the policeman she tried not to notice.

Fiona left Mags to her primping and peeked through the window in the door that separated the kitchen from the shop, scowling when she saw the officer leaning over the counter as he chatted up her aunt Bridget.

Case in point, the gaggle of groupies who followed him wherever he went was an annoyance she ignored whenever they took up valuable real estate from paying customers to ogle his rear end. And the way he batted those long, thick lashes and turned her whiskey-swilling, cigar-smoking, hard-as-nails aunty into a giggling schoolgirl? Absolutely revolting.

Bridget reached into the case and pulled out a chocolate-dipped shortbread. *Don't do it. Don't do it*, Fiona mentally screamed as Bridget slid the sweet treat across the counter with a wink and a smile.

Office Kilsgaard laughed as he accepted the cookie. The husky notes tickled Fiona's eardrums and made her right eye twitch. How could that man eat so many sweets and not appear to gain an ounce? Not even his bulky jacket could hide the bulging muscles of his arms and his flat, washboard stomach.

Nope, nope, nope. She closed her eyes to also ignore the way his tan uniform emphasized his strong thighs and finely sculpted backside. Khaki was not meant to be attractive.

When she risked opening her eyes, their gazes collided and he flashed her a dazzling smile. Crap. Now he caught her staring like a peeping Tom leering through a bedroom window. Perfect.

She willed the heat in her cheeks to subside and pushed open the door.

"Ah, here's the fair Fiona now. How are you this lovely morning?"

"Fine, thank you," she gritted out between a tight smile and concentrated on refilling the display of cookies as if it were brain surgery.

Unable to resist the allure, she sneaked a glance at his chiseled profile. God, it should be a crime to be that handsome. He was so beautiful, it hurt to look at him. A helicopter started in her tummy and her throat closed up. The tray of cookies rattled against where she rested it on the display as her brain misfired.

Agh! She mentally kicked herself. She hated feeling so clumsy and socially inept. It wasn't as if she were a femme fatale when it came to men, but usually she was able to keep better control of her faculties.

With a deep, calming breath, she turned her focus to the other customers in the shop. "Is there anything I can get anyone?"

Silence followed her query. Four pairs of eyes remained trained on Officer Dhavin, who was laughing at one of Bridget's dirty jokes.

"Hello? Joan? What can I get you?"

"What?" The other woman started and turned to Fiona with a girlish giggle. "Oh, um, I'm still looking. Right, ladies?"

Several absentminded nods followed.

"Uh-huh. All right. Well, let me know if I can assist anyone. I'll just keep putting these cookies away. But...you might want to place your order before Officer Dhavin snaps them all up. You know, they're his favorite," she finished with a conspiratorial whisper.

"I'll take a dozen."

"I'll take two."

"Oh, hey," Officer Dhavin objected when he spotted the frenzy at the counter. "Save some of those for me, ladies. I want a dozen too, Fiona. And a box of Rollo Eggs. I knew your shipment was arriving today. Those are the best."

"I'll take a box too," Joan piped up along with more raised hands.

Hmmm, perhaps having the officer around wasn't an altogether bad thing.

Fiona stifled a laugh as she imagined the signage she could create to place around the section of candies she special-ordered from England, complete with Officer Dhavin's sparkly white smile. Perhaps she should bump up the price a bit too.

"Thanks, *lebshone*," he said in his sinfully rich accent and Fiona felt the tic start back in her eye and her tongue fill her mouth.

The officer's family had recently settled in her tiny hamlet of Cedar from somewhere in Sweden, or so she'd been told, and his accent was a lyrical mix of grace and dominance that made her think of late nights and kinky sex.

Damn if she could figure out what it was about him that pushed her lascivious and annoyed buttons at the same time. His cousins, while incredibly handsome in their own right, never affected her as he did. All the members of the Kilsgaard clan had their own unofficial fan club, but Dhavin was the only one who made her sweat. However—a snort of laughter tickled her nose—heaven help her if she were to be in a room with all three of them at once. If the Vikings were anything like those three, no wonder they conquered the world so easily.

Officer Dhavin poked his nose into the bag and drew in the sugary scent. "You have the best sweets I've ever tasted. Except that one candy, what was it called? Plenty of Goodness? Yes, did not care for it."

Dear Lord, even his disgusted face was adorable.

Bridget laughed. "Not a fan of black licorice, eh?"

"Is that what that flavor is? I think I'd prefer to eat my boots."

The fan girls erupted into hysterical laughter and Fiona rolled her eyes so hard she saw spots.

"So, Fiona." He leaned his arm against the pastry case. "Have you been to the new casino yet? My cousin Amaryllis says the restaurant there is fantastic. Not as good as hers, or so she claims, but still excellent."

"No, I haven't."

And she left it at that, keeping her head down as she readied a box of inventory for display.

"Are you talking about Chinook's?" Mags came from Fiona's blindside and hip-checked her, sending a box of gold-foiled eggs flying. "I am dying to go eat there. It's the finest thing to hit town in forever, well, besides you, Officer."

Seriously? Seriously.

"You're a doll, Mags. Say, is that a new color of lip gloss you're wearing?"

The girl batted her lashes. "Aren't you sweet for noticing?"

Fiona restrained the urge to gag and stooped to pick up the dented chocolates. Mags had unbuttoned her blouse so low, the lace of her pink bra peeked out to frame the sideways smile of her cleavage. The tails of her shirt were tied to expose her flat midriff and a pink gem nestled in her navel.

It was difficult not to besmirch the twenty-one-year-old for having a body a Barbie doll would envy. The girl did have good genes. But Mags' size-four waist made Fiona woefully aware of her size-twelve middle. The only time she hated her shape was in the company of truly beautiful people, which pissed her off.

If she remained in their presence a second longer, she was going to embarrass herself, she just knew it.

She all but ran to the kitchen and attacked the stack of dishes in the sink as if they owed her money.

Stupid. It was all so stupid. The only person with the power to make her feel inferior was herself. And at times, she was so good at it, bullies could take lessons from her. Why should it matter to her that Officer Gorgeous liked the giggling woman-child type? It was none of her business. None at all.

"Fiona," Bridget called out in a stage whisper as she barreled through the doorway. "What are you doing?"

She held up a soapy scrub brush. "Mowing the lawn."

"Don't be a smartass. Get back out there this instant. Officer Dhavin was about to ask you out."

"Yeah, right. If he's going to ask anyone out, it'll be Mags and her perky breasts."

"Not if you're out there. Now go. He's the best catch in town, and if you don't make a move, someone else will. I tell you, if I was five years younger, I'd be after him myself."

"Only five?" she asked with a raised brow.

Bridget smiled sweetly and saluted her with a firmly raised middle finger. "What is the problem? You need a man."

"I don't need a man."

"You want a man."

"I don't—well, maybe. But I don't want him."

"Are you daft? What is wrong with that hunk-a-hunk of burning love?"

"Seriously? He flirts with *everyone*. Even with men. Have you seen how he walks into the room, flashes that big smile and bats those long lashes then gets whatever he wants? Even from you. How would I be able to trust that he's telling the truth and not just feeding me a lie? He's a player. And I don't trust players."

"Pish-tosh." Bridget waved her words away. "You don't know that."

"Remember when he went out with Janice Harbinger? She

kept going on and on about his skills in bed."

"Oh yeah." She giggled. "I remember that."

"And then two days later she went on and on about how he said they would be better off as friends."

"Oh yeah. I remember that too. But Janice Harbinger is a toad. She's plastic from the top of her weave to the ends of her fake nails. He probably realized that and got out when he could. At least he didn't string her along."

"Whatever. It's none of my business." She slid the rack of dirty dishes into the washer and pulled down the door. The roaring swish of water effectively blocked out any more of Bridget's argument.

At least for the three minutes it took for the washer to run.

As soon as the cycle completed, her aunt was at her side. "So, you're not even going to give him a chance?"

"At what? Laughing in my face? No way. I don't want a man who plays games. It's a waste of time. If a guy is interested in me, I want him to come up to me and say, 'Hi, I like you and I think we could have a great time together. How about next Friday?'"

"Or, you could do the same to a man you like."

Walk up to man and make herself vulnerable? Now that was pure crazy talk. Opening her own business, drag racing, even singing in public, no problem. Asking a guy out for a date? No way. Just call her chickenshit.

"I could do that," she hedged. "But as I said before, I'm not interested in Office Dhavin as anything more than a paying customer."

Bridget flapped her arms. "Balk-balk!"

"Don't we have other customers you can attend to? I'm sure Mags is otherwise occupied."

"I'll be praying for you, girlie," Bridget called out on her way to the front. "It's going to take a man from another planet to make you happy."

A thunderous boom rattled the windowpanes and the pots and pans hanging from the baker's rack clanged together.

"Dear heavens," Bridget shrieked.

Fiona ran to the front of the now-empty store and out onto the sidewalk where the other women gathered. Officer Dhavin was already halfway down the street, racing toward a cluster of people pointing and shouting.

Mags waved down a passing car. "Mrs. Anderson, did you see what happened?"

Mrs. Anderson rolled down the window and ran a shaking hand through her hair. "A logging truck lost its load and crushed some cars. At least that's what it looked like. I just missed getting pinned by some of the logs. Let me tell you, my life really did flash before my eyes."

"Is anyone hurt?" Fiona asked.

"I would be surprised if they weren't. Hopefully help comes quick and someone calls the Chameleon. They're gonna need his help."

All the women drew a collective breath.

"The Chameleon," Fiona whispered when her lungs regained their function.

At her words, the rest of the ladies ran down the street with Mags leading the charge.

Fiona took a step to follow and drew up short. What was she doing? She couldn't go running into the freezing cold to go gawk at a horrible accident. She wasn't even wearing a coat.

No, no, no, no. Mere moments ago she'd just been berating the women of Cedar for falling all over a man because he was handsome, and here she was, ready to do the same.

Of course, this wasn't just any man. It was the Chameleon. Courageous and kind. Mysterious and built, as her aunt would say, like a brick shithouse. Lord, did he have some muscles. And she really wanted to see him. Really, really wanted to see him.

Nope. She took a step toward the door. She was better than a crazed fan. Difficult though it was, she forced her legs to turn and go back into the shop. Perhaps one of her customers would come back with some juicy details. Secondhand knowledge would just have to satisfy her Chameleon craving.

Bridget stood in the doorway with a black coat in her hand. She pressed the garment into Fiona's arms. "Go. I'll watch the shop. And take pictures. Well, not of the accident, but you know."

Leave it to her aunt to push her across the line of proper to ill-advised. "Are you sure?"

"Yes. Go."

"Okay. But I'm not taking any pictures. That's just tacky."

A dozen others joined Fiona as she walked, not ran, down the street, passing the collection of shops that made up the core of the town that was founded on the backs of loggers and copper miners. Cedar was like any other town that was wedged between the old and the new. The city was a few hours journey down the mountain, and the dense forest of the Cascades provided a buffer from the fast-paced lifestyle that comes with city living. On the surface, Cedar wasn't that special, except when it came to one thing. Or rather, person.

It wasn't the potential carnage that drew Fiona and the nearby citizens to the scene of the accident, but the possibility of seeing *him*.

A good-sized crowd was already gathered at the intersection when she arrived, obscuring the view of the worst of the damage. Even on tiptoe, all she saw was the top of the jack-knifed trailer and massive jumble of logs that looked like a giant dropped a box of oversized Lincoln Logs.

"Fiona! Up here," came a voice from the left.

She turned to see Mags waving from the top of the play area across the street. Fiona wove through the crush of people to the big toy and warily eyed the metal ladder. Condensation covered the rungs and were icy cold as she wrapped her fingers around the rod.

"I don't think my insurance covers falling from a jungle gym," she muttered.

"Just don't look down." Mags threw open her arms to encompass the view when Fiona reached the top. "Isn't this the dopest spot?"

"Dope. Right." Fiona caught her breath and clung on to the railing as she squeezed onto the platform with Mags and three other ladies. "Is this sturdy for so many adults?"

Mags blew her a raspberry. "He's not here yet. But he will be. I just know it."

From their perch Fiona was able to see more of the wreckage and cringed over being there to witness the spectacle. Prudence urged her to go back, but her inner teenager kept her feet in place as if she were waiting to see her favorite rock star bolt out of the back of an arena, and nobody, not even the braless bimbo with the fake tan and miniskirt was going to push her from her primo location.

Only there were no bimbos gawking at the accident, just soccer moms, business owners and police. Oh, and Janice Harbinger. Correction. There was one bimbo.

The chaos surrounding the scene was movie-quality surreal. It appeared that the logging truck tried to take the corner too sharply, tipping enough to throw off its balance. The resulting shift in weight broke the bindings on the multi-ton load. The spill of logs caught two cars, crushing them against the side of the nearby building.

"Geez Louise." Fiona whistled and kept her gaze off the worst of the wreckage. "Is anyone hurt?"

Mags shrugged. "Haven't heard. The police arrived just as you did, but Officer Dhavin has been trying to get to the drivers."

Fiona followed the direction Mags pointed in and saw Officer Dhavin searching for a way to relieve the pressure and get the occupants out of their smashed vehicles. Meanwhile, more officers set up barricades and were trying their best to push the onlookers back.

Suddenly a ripple of energy ran up her spine and the crowd began to vibrate as they all felt the surge.

"I see him," someone shouted and all attention was shifted to a black blur and a swirl of mist barreling down the street.

The whirling mass stopped and there he was. The Chameleon.

No one knew who he was or where he came from, only that he definitely wasn't local. And by local, that meant of the entire planet Earth. He swooped in when people had need and left just as fast, never asking for anything in return. He was Superman and Spiderman rolled into one delicious hunk of man.

Fiona had only seen him from afar on a few occasions, and he wore a cowl that covered his head, so she didn't know what he looked like, or even what color his eyes were. But he had one of those chiseled, manly chins, and lips that looked as if one kiss would be so powerful, it could straighten her hair.

And that body...my oh my. Tightly muscled with lightning-quick reflexes, he was strong enough to bench-press a car. And he had too. He once pulled a school bus to safety that had slid off the end of a bridge during a flash flood.

Besides his incredible strength, he also had super speed,

which made her wonder if he was super everywhere. Man, there were parts of him she wanted to dip in chocolate and lick clean.

Stretched across his broad chest was a tunic made from some type of mystical fabric that shimmered silver one moment then blended in with the environment the next, hence the nickname, the Chameleon.

Fiona sucked on her bottom lip as she watched him speak with Sheriff Briggs and Officer Dhavin. What did his voice sound like? Was it deep and raspy? Did he have an accent? Was he as quiet as he was humble, or were there moments he revealed a playful side? Did he have a family, friends? A girlfriend?

So much about him was a mystery, which was part of his appeal. In Fiona's mind, he was the perfect fantasy lover, kind of like crushing on a famous actor. He'd treat her like a princess and never give her cause to cry.

The roar of fire engines sent heat streaking across her cheeks. She pressed her frozen fingers to her face and mentally groaned.

What was she doing? Lives were in danger and here she was mentally undressing a stranger and indulging in wicked thoughts. She was so going to burn in hell for this.

DHAVIN TRIED TO shake off the wave of lust that slipped down his spine and grabbed him by the balls, but the ache wouldn't ease. People's lives were at stake, yet he couldn't think beyond the sweet throb that made his cock as hard as the baton at his hip.

"Officer Kilsgaard, are you listening?" Sheriff Brett Briggs asked. The stern snap in her voice broke through his haze.

He sucked in a bracing breath and turned toward the sheriff. "Ya. You said the tow trucks will be here in ten minutes."

She frowned, obviously not believing his lie for a second. "Are you all right?"

"I'm fine." He pulled the wide strap of his gun belt down to cover his erection.

His cousin Kristos, aka the Chameleon, chuckled and leaned close to whisper in their native language, "It's a good thing she can't sense emotions like we can. She'd make you be the Chameleon all the time if she knew how some of these women felt about her husband."

Brett clicked her tongue at them. "You do know Amaryllis is teaching me Skandavian? Soon you won't be able to talk around me." She smiled sweetly. "Now, if we can get back to the task at hand."

Dhavin nodded but his attention drifted back to the sea of emotions rising from the gathering crowd. The appearance of the Chameleon always inspired a mixture of reactions from awe to curiosity, as well as admiration and a high level of desire from the female population.

But today there was a headier sensation in the air. A sense of longing that was dark and rich, like a chocolate from his favorite sweet shop, and the sensation thickened his blood. He looked over his shoulder and spotted the source of the sweetness standing on the top of a child's play structure.

Fiona Corrione.

Owner of the Sugared Thistle Candy and Bakery, and from the moment he first saw her two months ago, the star of his wickedest fantasies.

He couldn't name exactly what it was about her that fascinated him, but all he wanted to do was scoop her up and carry her away to where he could caress every inch of her soft skin and make her cry out his name as he gave her orgasm after crashing orgasm.

And she hated him.

Well, maybe hate was too strong a word, but she definitely didn't like him. His knowledge of American slang was feeble at best, but the conversation he overheard her have with her aunt earlier did not sound encouraging. And he'd be damned if he knew why she felt that way.

He was always friendly to her, gave her lots of compliments, and spent a good chunk of his paycheck at her store. He had so many of her confections, he had to tack twenty miles to his morning run to burn the extra calories. Yet nothing he did eased the wariness he sensed coming from her whenever he approached. On the outside she'd smile and be the epitome of politeness, but she'd watch him like one does a cat that allows you to pet them yet has a history of rearing back and biting at a moment's provocation.

What did he have to do to have her look at him the way

she was looking at his cousin right now? Standing on that structure, she was like a character out of one of the epic human novels he read on his journey to Earth. The wind played with the loose curls that escaped her bun, and her cheeks and nose were the most charming shade of pink. The soft pad of her lower lip was trapped between her white teeth and those chocolate eyes shimmered with heated thoughts he'd give his trusted sword to know.

"Are you coming or not?"

He jerked at the shout. "What?"

The cutouts in Kristos' mask highlighted his narrowed stare and downturned mouth. "What is wrong with you? There are people we need to save, or is there somewhere more important you need to be at this time, *botjka*?"

"Fuck off, *Chameleon*. I'm right behind you." He didn't need his cousin calling him an inept, untried virgin warrior to add to the injury he nursed from Fiona's coldness.

He joined Kristos at the front of the big rig and pointed to a cross-section of logs. "That area right there concerns me the most. If we lift the logs in the wrong order, the rest will come crashing down. Can you move fast enough and not be crushed into the side of the building?"

"I guess we'll find out." Kristos placed his foot on the grill, ready to climb.

Dhavin stopped him with a hand on his shoulder. "Careful."

"Thank you," Kristos said with a grin. They may cut each

other down on occasion, but blood was blood and family meant everything.

The Chameleon scaled up the side of the trailer and began to carefully pluck the thousand-pound-a-piece logs as if they were kindling and dropped them to the asphalt below. Each resulting boom as wood smacked into ground made Dhavin flinch and emphasized the seriousness of the situation.

Two tow trucks arrived and Dhavin waved one to the front of the accident where he stood and the second around the back to where Officer Reutgers hung half in and half out of the broken back window of an SUV, tending to a victim.

Dhavin waved to the woman huddled in the driver's seat of the car on his end. "Hang tight, Ms. Shurgard. We'll have you out soon."

She gave him a weak nod and sank farther into her seat, curling into a tight ball and warily watching the roof above her creak and moan as the weight crushing the car was lessened.

He accepted a hook from the tow truck driver and crawled under the vehicle and attached it to the front axle. The sound of shifting timber encouraged him to work quickly and shimmy out to a safer location. He climbed back to his feet and reached for his radio. "Ready. Reutgers, you secure?"

"We have a go. In three. Three. Two. One."

Dhavin waved the go-ahead for the driver to start pulling, and he heard the wrecker on the other side begin to drag its load. The scrape of wood on metal made his teeth ache. As the cars began to move, the blockage of logs shuddered.

"Chameleon," Dhavin shouted. "We have to move."

Kristos nodded and stepped up his movements.

The SUV cleared the barricade sooner than the sedan, tipping the rest of the load in Dhavin's direction. A log with the diameter of a big-wheel tire slid toward his head. With lightning-fast reflexes, he threw up his hand, stopping its momentum an inch from his nose.

His arm trembled under the weight as he held the avalanche up so the sedan could continue its slow slide to safety. Sweat rolled down his face as his muscles spasmed with the exertion.

"Come on. Come on," he muttered through tightly clenched teeth.

With a grunt, he kicked at the bumper, sending it skidding the last several feet before he dropped his hand and leapt to the side.

The ground trembled and a tremendous dust cloud arose, obscuring all vision as timber crashed to the road.

Dhavin swatted at the bits of flying wood splinters. "Is everyone all right?"

Brett ran to his side. "Were you hit?"

"No. I am good. Is everyone clear?"

"Yeah. Barely. Smooth move there." Her features tightened as her eyes widened and her pointed glare went to the car with the boot-sized dent in its bumper.

"Just performing my duty, ma'am."

All around them the crowd cheered and waved their arms.

Their elation raised the hair on his neck and made him feel like he was floating on air. He helped to save the day, yet no one was looking in his direction. Following their gaze, he spotted the Chameleon on the roof, one hand lifted in acknowledgment of their praise. Kristos nodded once then fled, skipping from rooftop to rooftop away from the scene.

Disappointment settled on Dhavin's shoulders. If this had been his day off, he'd be the one in the suit receiving all the accolades and being called hero instead of his cousin.

Hell, he didn't begrudge Kristos of the attention. When he wore the mask, his efforts were just as celebrated. But today the praise for his cousin bothered him. More specifically, the praise of one person.

Fiona was jumping up and down, her hands cupped to her mouth, shouting her jubilation. Even at this distance he could see the sparkle in her eyes.

That was what he wanted. He wanted her to look at him as if he were her hero.

"Come on." Brett slapped him on the back. "Let's start directing the cleanup so we can head home."

Home.

The word went right into his ear and struck a nerve that made the muscles in his jaw clench.

Home for the time being was living in his cousin Lucian's former room at the house of their adopted Earth-uncle. It was comfortable and Uncle Harlan was an easy man to live with, but it wasn't really a home. Not like what Kristos had with

Brett, or Lucian had with his wife Amaryllis. He was missing the hearth to his home.

Ahh.

The realization struck him dumb for a moment. So there was the cause of his discontent. He was lonely. Not in the physical sense, but emotionally. He wanted a woman of his own, and not just any woman, a true partner, his other half.

As a *Llanos* warrior on his home planet of Skandavia, he hadn't given much thought to having a family of his own. He had been the head of Princess Amaryllis' guard and as such her safety and comfort had been his only priority. A wife and resulting offspring would have been left on their own, a price he could never ask a female to pay. The occasional affair sated his physical needs and they had been enough, for he had been resigned to his fate. It was a privilege, and one he had fought hard for, to be a member of the royal guard.

Then the revolution happened. Amaryllis had been sent to Earth in exile and his world had been upended. The enemy would have been defeated if not for the compassionate heart of his queen. The concussive wave caused by her murder rippled out in a tsunami-like wave that destroyed the *Llanos* family.

But with destruction came new and unexpected opportunities. Now his future was an open plane and fantasies he never entertained were a possibility, like a bonded mate.

He looked in the direction of the dispersing crowd, a magnetic pull beckoned him to follow.

Was his mate out there right now? Was she so close he

could smell the sweetness of her skin if he inhaled hard enough?

The scent of cooked sugar and chocolate filled his nose as he drew a deep breath. A few blocks away, he saw the back of Fiona's head as she talked with Mags.

A smile flirted with his lips. Perhaps another trip to the candy store was in order.

Chapter Two

D HAVIN KNOCKED ON the door to Brett's office. "If you no longer have need of me, I will be departing now."

"One second." She finished typing the sentence she was working on then lifted her gaze from the monitor. "We're covered, but thanks for asking. Good work today, by the way. You know, I wasn't sure how you'd take to being a cop, if you'd find it challenging enough. Especially after you've guarded royalty and fought revolutionaries, but we do have our moments of excitement around here, and let me tell you, having you here has set the example to the others. For that alone, I owe you big."

"It's my pleasure," he said with a slight bow. "I live to serve the people, and you are a leader worth following."

The corner of her mouth quirked up. Brett knew she was the best sheriff Cedar ever had, but it had been a struggle to earn her men's respect. Once she established she was a force to be reckoned with, no one questioned her abilities. However Dhavin sensed she was still hesitant to accept praise, even from family.

"Have good night, Sheriff."

"You too."

He turned to leave but held back. His thoughts of the day came back to poke at his conscience. "Brett, can I ask you a question?"

"Sure."

"What does the word player mean?"

She frowned. "Can you use it in a sentence?"

He took a breath. "That man is a player."

The frown melted as her jade eyes sparkled with laughter. She tilted her head back and let loose with a big belly laugh.

Now it was his turn to frown. He stepped deeper into the room and closed the door. Why did he think he didn't want whatever she was about to say to be overheard. "What is so humorous?"

She wiped at her eyes. "Let me guess. You've found the first woman who's immune to your *Llanos* charm?"

For a human, his cousin-in-law had a frighteningly high level of empathetic powers.

"Then I am correct in thinking that it's a negative term."

"A player is a person, usually a man, who treats dating like a game and moves from woman to woman in the pursuit of sex."

He sat heavily in the chair across from her desk. "That doesn't describe me at all."

"Well…" She bit her lip. "I can see how you might be thought of that way."

"What are you talking about? Since I've come to Earth I've

courted only one woman from this town."

She raised a blonde brow. "And what about the women at Amaryllis' club?"

Of course she'd bring *that* up. "I would be beyond stunned if the people of Cedar knew about The Cavern and the activities that transpire there. Besides, I haven't been there in months. The novelty of sampling a variety of women at the snap of my fingers grew old very quickly. Regardless, I have done nothing to establish such a reputation."

"You are an outrageous flirt," Brett shot back before he finished his sentence.

"A what?"

"Flirt. You're extra nice to women. You give them lots of compliments and make them think they're special."

What was she talking about? "And that's a bad thing? I have noticed the women of this colony have very low opinions of themselves for no reason. By telling a woman she is beautiful, she will feel beautiful and therefore will become beautiful. How can that be wrong?"

Her smile was genuine, but gave him the impression she was indulging him. "It's not wrong, to a point. I don't know how people behaved on your home planet, but on Earth, especially America, when a man compliments a woman it usually indicates that he is romantically interested in her. We don't have the advantage of being able to use empathic abilities to differentiate between someone who is being polite and someone who is looking for a more intimate interaction."

"I still do not understand."

She chewed on her lip and held out her hands. "Okay, so you're a military guy. When you were in training I'm sure everyone was treated the same. You all failed or succeeded as one unit, correct?"

"Ya."

"But then you were promoted over all the others. You were singled out and acknowledged for your skills. How did that make you feel?"

"I felt great. Accomplished."

"Now let's equate this to women. You treat all women with the same courtesy, which is over and above what other men do on a normal basis. The one woman you are actually interested in isn't going to notice you're into her. How can she feel extra-special when you treat her the same as other women?"

He sat back in his seat. "Ah, I think I see now. I need to turn down the compliments in casual conversation and turn them up when I'm with her."

"Exactly."

Could the answer be so simple? He rose to his feet with a renewed sense of hope. "Thank you, Brett. I didn't think Earth would be so complicated to traverse. I appreciate your council. Kristos is lucky to have you by his side as an advisor."

She laughed so hard, she snorted. "Can you please remind him of that?"

"I will do so, often. Have a good night."

"You too," she said with a smile that suggested she knew

his route home was going to take a detour.

The Sugared Thistle was a convenient five blocks away from the police station, a distance that could have taken him the blink of an eye to travel, but he took his time, needing the scarce few minutes to compose what he wanted to say to Fiona.

She said it herself that morning that she appreciated a man who was straightforward and direct with his intentions. He thought he had been, but now that he replayed their earlier encounters, he had kept his conversation in the friendly range in deference to the nervousness he always sensed from her whenever they were together. If she wanted a take-charge man, he was definitely qualified.

The door to the Mediterranean restaurant opened and out spilled all twelve members of the Cedar Ladies Bridge Club. Their laughter tickled over his skin like seltzer water. He pulled the hood of his windbreaker farther down over his face and skirted past the group before they could stop him with conversation. From experience he knew they could talk about any subject for hours.

He reached the door to the import store just as Fiona was turning the sign in the window to *Closed*. When she looked up at his hooded face she jumped back with a startled gasp. He flipped back his hood and her look of surprise shifted to an unease of a different sort.

She opened the door and motioned him in.

"Hello, Fiona. I've come—"

"For your chocolate."

"My what?"

She stepped behind the counter and retrieved a bag. "Bridget found the chocolate you left behind earlier. She thought you might be back for it."

"Oh, thank you." He shifted the white paper bag from one hand to the other. He wasn't expecting to have to hold a prop.

Fiona rocked on her heels and looked everywhere around the room but at him as silence fell between them.

What was wrong with him? Never before had he been so tongue-tied, especially around a female. Where was his legendary charm now? As the quietness continued, he realized they were the only souls in the shop. While that worked in his favor for his plans of courtship, who was there to protect her from late-hour assailants?

"Is it just you here?"

She nodded.

"Is that safe? Who's going to protect you if you have an intruder?"

Her eyebrows rose. "There aren't that many people looking to knock over a sweet shop. Normally there are two of us here, but business was slow. It usually is when it starts raining in the late afternoon, so I let Mags go home early."

"Who's going to escort you to your vehicle?"

A grin flirted with her lips. "I can walk the five feet to my car on my own."

"Unacceptable. I will wait until you are finished and ensure you make it to your car safely."

"That's not necessary."

"I insist." Why hadn't he realized the risk she took closing up the store in the dark winter nights on her own? Mental note. More nightly patrols of the neighborhood during closing hours.

"I'm sure you have better things to do than wait for me to mop the floors."

"It is not an issue. I'll even help." After setting his bag on the counter, he picked up a table with one hand and two chairs in the other, moving them to the side of the room.

"Well, aren't you handy?" She disappeared through the doorway to the kitchen and came back rolling a bucket filled with purple water. She began in the corner closest to the front door and moved the mop with a smooth back-and-forth motion that spoke of her experience wielding the implement. "So... Will this be your first winter in the Northwest?"

Did his ears just deceive him? Fiona was initiating a conversation? Perhaps wooing her was not going to be as difficult as he thought. "Ya, but compared to winters back home, whatever your weather throws my way will feel tropical."

"That cold in Sweden, huh? I don't mind the rain here so much, but the gray can get really oppressive. That's why my parents and brother moved to Phoenix. Soak up some vitamin D and lounge by the pool. They love it there, but pool attire is not really my style. Have you been south at all?"

"No. I've been to the city, but that's all I've been able to see of America." He shifted the furniture around as she worked, easily anticipating her needs before she directed. "I'd like to see more and explore. Especially if I have the right person to show me around."

"I'm sure you'll have plenty of volunteers."

There was an odd note in her tone that deflated his earlier elation and urged him to get right to the point of his visit.

"Fiona. Would you like to accompany me to dinner this Friday?"

She paused then looked up at him with a wrinkled brow. "Who's all going?"

"It will be just you and me."

"Oh." She worried that full lower lip and strangled the mop handle. "No, thank you."

He waited, but then she returned to her task as if that was the end of the conversation. No way he was going to leave her rejection at that. "Why not?"

"I know my aunt probably pressured you to ask me out. She thinks a woman can't be happy unless she's in a relationship. I can let her know that you did the nice thing and offered, so don't worry about her bothering you about it again."

"She didn't pressure me. I want to go out with you."

"That's okay. I get it. You and I don't orbit in the same circles. It was sweet of you to try to make my aunt happy. You're a nice guy, very popular. There are at least a couple dozen women you would have a better time with than me."

The more she talked, the faster she moved, mopping herself right out of the room. The salty-sour taste of her embarrassment coated his tongue. How could she think that he had to be persuaded to spend time with her?

"Fiona, this has nothing to do with your aunt." He followed her squeaky trail and caught up with her near the cleaning closet. "Why don't you believe me?"

"Because I'm me and you're you, and I know she thinks I need to find a real man instead of fantasizing about the one I can't have."

There was another? His breath caught at the thought. "Who?"

She avoided the question by bending over to tilt the bucket of dirty water into the low utility basin. He lifted the container with ease and tipped it the rest of the way for her.

"Whoa, you're huge," he heard her murmur under her breath.

He looked down at her and realized how much smaller she was than he. This was the first time she stood before him without a counter or table between them. The top of her head reached him mid-chest and her eyes were as large as chocolate chip cookies as she stared up, way up at him and visually measured the breadth of his shoulders as he unintentionally trapped her in the corner.

He stepped back so as not to overwhelm her. "I would like to know who this competitor for your affections is, especially if he is too stupid to have made a bid for your hand already."

A crooked grin touched her lips. "Are you for real? I don't know anyone who talks like you do." She took the bucket from him and retreated to the closet, releasing a small sigh once she increased the distance between them.

"English is not my native tongue, and you're avoiding the question."

"I don't want to discuss this with you. It's silly and you'll think I am the stupid one."

"I will not think you are stupid."

"Why not? The man doesn't know I exist and I know nothing about him. Nothing. Not even the color of his eyes or hair. I don't even know if he has hair. How ridiculous is that?" She dropped her head and bit her lip as she swirled the mop across the floor. "But I can't stop thinking about him, and until that stops, no one else compares. Not even you, who is like the second most gorgeous man in Cedar."

That made him smile. She thought he was good-looking? At least that gave him something to work with. "Second?"

"He comes first. And your cousins are taken. I don't crush on men in committed relationships, even in my imagination. Look, just forget I said anything. Please."

How is it she knew this man was attractive, yet so little else about his appearance. Oh-ho!

If Amaryllis had been there, she would have smacked him in the head and shouted one of her favorite American collo-quialisms, "Well, duh."

"It's the Chameleon, isn't it?" he asked, half afraid to hope.

The pink flush racing across her cheeks was his answer. She busied herself by untying the apron around her waist and hanging it on its designated peg, arranging the fabric until it fell to her precise specifications.

Why hadn't he realized her desire for his alter ego had gone behind simple lustful appreciation? This was good. Maybe not exactly as he planned, but he could make this work in his favor.

"I can see why you find him interesting. I think most of the women in this town think he's fascinating."

"Don't remind me," she muttered.

He leaned against the butcher block table with feigned casualness. "So what is it about him that keeps you up at nights? How do you know he's worth your affections?"

"Are you kidding?" She continued to look away as she pulled on her coat and gathered her purse. "He's kind and compassionate. He takes action when needed but he can take direction too, you know, from the sheriff or the fire captain, which means he's willing to work with others. He's humble, well, most of the time. Lately..." She frowned and shook her head.

What? What? "Lately..." he repeated.

She shrugged. "I don't know. It just seems like lately he's been a bit showy."

Alarm straightened his spine. "Showy? I do not know this word."

"Like showboating. Showing off his talents for attention.

He used to appear on the scene, do his thing and then leave with a little wave once the day was saved. But recently I've noticed he amps up the applause, egging on the crowd. Kind of like he's getting off on the attention."

"Is that wrong? Maybe he thinks the people want more of him."

"What more could they want? He risks his life for them all the time. I like him when he's humble. Like today."

Mental note—don't sign autographs. "If you are interested in him, why don't you let him know?"

She burst out laughing as she opened the back door and waited for him to exit before locking it shut. "Yeah, like I know where he lives or hangs out. And as you've said, he has a lot of admirers. Trust me, the interest will only be one-sided."

"You don't know that. I'm interested in you. Please go out with me this weekend?"

Over their heads a streetlamp flickered, casting half her face in shadow. She took a deep breath and let it out in a slow, billowy cloud. "I can't. Look, thank you for asking, but I'm very aware of who I am. I'm the stay-at-home-with-a-good-book kind of girl and you're adrenaline and adventure. I'd bore you to tears. Guys like you don't have happily-ever-afters with girls like me." Her voice cracked and she looked away as a shimmer glistened in her eyes. "Thank you for walking me to my car. Have a good night, Office Kilsgaard."

As she raced the few steps to her vehicle, a sharp ache filled the spot in his chest between his two hearts. Now he understood. She didn't think she was worthy. The fear she harbored of being hurt reached out like a mystical hand to tighten around his throat. With his powers he picked up the incessant warning for her to hold her desires in check. If she didn't go after what she wanted, she wouldn't get hurt.

What had happened in her past to give her such a low opinion of herself? Nothing in his conversations with her aunt indicated a great heartache in Fiona's life, but something had made an impression.

After a quick glance around to ensure he was alone, he shimmied up the lamppost and adjusted the flickering light to constantly illuminate the parking area, then jumped down with thoughts of Fiona racing through his mind.

He needed a new approach to get her to take a chance on them. Words were only words, but actions spoke volumes.

A smile stretched his lips as a plan took shape. She may not listen to him, but there was one person she would most definitely believe.

Chapter Three

"**E**ARTH TO FIONA." Mags clapped her hands in front of Fiona's nose. "You've washed that rack of dishes three times now."

"Oh geez." Fiona pulled on the arm of the industrial dishwasher and slid out the steaming tray full of mixing bowls and spatulas. The hot metal scorched her fingertips as she put them away.

"You've been spacey all day. Are you all right?"

"Yeah, just been thinking."

Contemplating was more like it. The previous night's conversation with Officer Kilsgaard wouldn't let her rest. Instead of a peaceful night's sleep, her imagination kept her awake with thoughts of painting his chest in caramel and licking him clean.

It had been easier to not think of him in a sexual way when she knew she had no chance of gaining his interest. But now, oh now, there was the possibility and never was there a more dangerous concept. Possibilities meant there was hope and hope could be doused as quickly as a match under a waterfall.

Was she completely insane turning down his eloquent request for a date? Really, what was the worst that could happen?

Well, she could fall in love with him, begin making plans for the future then have him dump her, leaving her as the newest Janice Harbinger of Cedar. Lovely.

Mags hung up her apron and reached for her coat. "Fiona, honey, do you want to talk about it?"

Yeah, like that was a brilliant idea. Not. Mags was already moody because Officer Kilsgaard hadn't asked her out the day before. This particular can of worms was best left sealed tightly closed.

"No, I'm good, really. Thanks for asking. Hey, can you take that box of unsold cookies by the fire station on your way home? If it's not a bother."

She snorted a short laugh. "Are you kidding? It will be my pleasure. Do you know how popular I'll be taking sweets to those hunky guys? Maybe I'll leave with a date."

"How do you do it?" Fiona couldn't help to ask. "I mean, how can you just put yourself out there like that with men? Doesn't it suck being heartbroken?"

Mags paused with her scarf in her hand. She slowly wound it around her neck as her eyes flickered with thought. "Yeah, it sucks, but at least I tried. I don't know. I like being in a relationship. Maybe I like it too much, which would explain why I keep going after the wrong guys. I settle for the next one instead of waiting for the right one. Men are like shoes. They may look great on the shelf, but until you try them on, you don't know if they'll make you look great or break your ankle if you take the wrong step."

"That makes too much sense." Fiona smiled for the first time that day.

"I do have my moments. But seriously. Men are stupid. Sometimes you have to make the first move or else they'll sit on their hands forever. Their caveman instinct has been drummed out of them by the feminist movement. Now we have to do everything."

"Wow, Mags, I wish I was as brave as you."

"Brave? Me? I'd say I'm more blissfully ignorant. If I think about it too much, I probably would stay home all of the time, wear turtleneck sweaters that go up to my eyeballs and take care of twenty cats. But I don't like cats, so out into the world I go."

Well, Fiona didn't have the cats, but there were a few high-neck sweaters in her closet. Oh God, she was going to become the crazy cat lady.

"Actually, Fiona, I admire how you don't go out with a bunch of guys. You know what you want and you don't deviate from that path."

"Thanks, I think."

"Do you want to take the cookies to the fire station? There are a few new recruits who looked pretty cute." She wiggled her eyebrows.

"No, you can have first pick. Besides, what would I have in common with a young fireman?"

"More than you think, boss lady. You're a pretty good

catch." She pulled her scarf over the lower portion of her face. "Have a good night."

"You too. Drive safe."

Fiona tugged on her coat and slung her purse over her shoulder as she turned off light switches on her way to the door. Could she borrow a page from Mags and take a chance on Officer Kilsgaard? Dhavin. If she was going to entertain the notion of a date, she had to start thinking of him as a man with a first name.

A laugh lodged in her throat and her skin tingled. As if she could forget he was a man.

Don't think about it. Don't think about it.

Like Mags said, if she thought about the pitfalls, she'd chicken out. Once she got home she'd find his phone number in her client files and give him a call...after a glass, or two, or three, of wine.

As she stepped outside a brisk wind barreled down the alley. Holy geez. She shivered and drew her arms in tight, that was icy. Winter had officially arrived, as much as she tried to ignore the signs of frosted windows and day after day of gray skies. The weather forecast called for a chance of snow. She hated snow. Snow meant bad roads, dented fenders and no customers.

She blew on her palms, tossing her keys from one hand to the other as she minded her steps on the slick asphalt.

"Oh shoot," she muttered as the keys slipped out of her hand and skidded across the ground.

She crouched down and squinted into the absolute dark-ness. She reached under the car and felt along the ground blindly. "Come on. Come on."

"Do you wish to be attacked? You make a tempting target."

She shot up to a stand and jumped back with a scream as a human figure landed before her in a smooth crouch.

"Sorry," the man said. "I did not mean to startle you."

"How did you think I'd react?" she snapped and blinked hard to erase the flash of fear from her vision. "Oh my God."

It was him. The Chameleon. Standing right in front of her. As large as a mountain and with biceps as big as watermelons. He wore his customary uniform of a fitted black long-sleeve shirt that stretched where he bulged, and the ever-present cowl covered his face. Standing so close to his magnificence, she could now make out the scalelike pattern of his tunic. The iridescent material shimmered and flattened as he moved. From far away he was an impressive sight, but in such close proximity he literally struck her dumb.

"Maybe you needed to be frightened." He took a step clos-er. "I heard this area might be prone to criminal activity and here I find a delicate young lady alone, in the dark, practically asking to be mugged, or worse. Just what were you doing?"

"I dropped. Keys," she managed to mumble as she pointed to the car.

His lips quirked a bit with a grin that deepened the dimple near the right corner of his mouth. "May I?"

May he what? Oh. She stepped back and stared at the wide

expanse of his back as he bent to retrieve her keys. Man, she could roll out two batches of cinnamon rolls across that much surface. When he straightened, she snapped her mouth closed and prayed there wasn't drool running down her chin.

"Here you go." He placed the keys into her palm. The metal was warm from the heat of his hand. "What's your name?"

"I'm—uh…" Holy crap. What was her name? "I—oh, I'm Fiona. Fiona."

"It's nice to meet you, Fiona." The black fabric around his eyes made the flecks of gold in the honey-brown irises look electrified.

"Brown," she whispered. What an unusual shade of brown they were too.

"What?"

"Nothing."

His smile broadened. "Fiona. I've heard of you. I'm told that to sample your sweets is like tasting a slice of heaven."

Oh the sweets she wanted him to sample.

She wrenched her mind from the gutter and focused on not continuing her spot-on impersonation of a major idiot. "Thank you. Can I get you anything? I have scone mix all scaled out and can whip up a batch right quick. Or candy. I have lots of chocolate-covered caramels made."

"I wouldn't want you to go to any trouble, but thank you for the offer. I think it's best to get you in your vehicle and send you safely on your way. It's too cold of a night to be outside."

"Why are you out then? And without a coat. Aren't you freezing?"

"Hold up your hand," he said with a secret smile that made her heart pound in her chest.

She lifted her hand and held her breath as he pressed his palm to hers. "You're so warm." She marveled at the amount of heat his skin generated. It was so toasty, she wanted to step into his arms and wrap him around her like a Snuggie.

"Where I come from is much colder than here. A night like this I consider to be overcast. There are people, like you, who need protection and so I am out to do what I can. But believe me, I'd rather be indoors in front of a fire with a good book and a mug of coffee right now."

"That sounds lovely."

"It would be even nicer to have someone to share a blanket with. Do you have anyone waiting for you at home?"

"No, I'm single. Very single."

"That was a trick question. You shouldn't admit those things to a stranger. What if I meant you harm and you've now confirmed no one is waiting for you?"

"You wouldn't hurt me."

"No, but you never know. I'm going to have to keep a closer eye on you."

"Seriously, I can take care of myself. You're very overwhelming, and I have to admit, I can't seem to form a sentence with you standing so close."

"I'm sorry." He took a step back.

"No!" She grabbed him by the tunic and hauled him closer. "Your heat feels nice."

His low chuckle was just as warm. "Perhaps we can continue this conversation another time when we're not in a dark, cold alley?"

"You want to see me again? I mean, not see me, see me, but see me?"

"Ah, Fiona, you make me laugh." He trailed the tip of his finger down her cheek and along her jaw. "You're like a cloud of cotton candy on a rainy day. Light, sweet and happy. I think you may be just what I've been looking for."

Her breath caught as the hot pad of his thumb brushed along her skin and skimmed her lower lip. His gorgeous eyes blurred in and out of focus as she swayed on her feet.

"Breathe, Fiona," he whispered.

"What?" She sucked in a cold breath. "Right. I'm all right."

He chuckled and took the keys from her hand to unlock the car door. "Let's get you inside and on your way. We'll meet again. I promise."

If she were smooth, she would have taken extra care to brush up against him. But she wasn't. She barely managed to take the few steps around the door and fall hard into the driver's seat.

"Thanks," she said as she regained possession of her keys.

"Good night, sweet Fiona." He brought her hand to his lips and brushed a scorching kiss against her knuckles and an answering burning ignited between her thighs.

Sweet. He called her sweet. She wanted to giggle, but stopped short of following the foolish reaction. "Good night, Chameleon."

He straightened with a sharp jerk. "Please, call me…Cam."

"Cam." Nicknames already. She loved it. "Take care of yourself as well."

He shut the door and waved as she pulled out of the parking space. In the rearview mirror he was a mythical figure, tall and imposing as he stood under the lamplight with tiny stars sparking off his tunic.

She kept her gaze on him until she was forced to turn the corner. Only then did her lungs begin to function properly and all of the blood rushed to her cheeks.

He wanted to see her again. Her. Fiona Corrione.

The little voice in the back of her mind whispered that this nice-guy routine might be his MO in bagging gullible women, but her heart whipped the notion into submission. She never heard of anyone being on a first-name basis with him. He had to be genuine.

The peal of laughter she tried to squelch burst forth. He wanted to see her!

Oh, there was so much to do. A haircut was first and foremost in order. Maybe she should pick up a good facial scrub at the store before heading home.

The snick of a memory dampened her excitement. Wasn't she supposed to do something when she got home?

Right, she was going to call someone, but dang if she could

remember who or what for.

She shrugged. It must not have been too important.

✦   ✦   ✦

SHE WANTED HIM.

Dhavin ran through the forest with light steps, leaping into the air to slap a jubilant high-five at the drippy tree branches.

Fiona wanted him. Well, not him specifically, but a part of him. She talked with him, smiled, trembled—she actually trembled when he held her hand. The lingering effects of her arousal still swirled through his mind, and his skin buzzed as if covered with a low-volt current.

A teeny-tiny part of his conscience itched at the dishonesty of his appearance in her life, but he'd take whatever he could get. If things between them worked out while under the guise of the Chameleon, then he'd explain everything, and she would be so in love with him it wouldn't matter that they met in slightly less than honest circumstances.

Love?

The thought made him slow to a stop. Was he already thinking of sentiments so profound? Yes, Fiona interested him like no other woman and the idea of having a wife tickled his conscience more and more every day, but entertaining the notion was entirely different than actively pursuing a mate. And tonight was the first time Fiona looked at him with something besides wariness. Love was a monumental leap from infatuation, and for a Skandavian, encompassed more than humans experienced. To meld his emotions with Fiona, he'd be entrusting her with all his secrets, as would she with him, whether she knew it or not.

Of course, there was always the option to not bond.

Hmm. He sat upon a rock and stroked his chin to contemplate this potentially land mine-laden field some more.

Back home many couples married and built families much the same way as the people on Earth, and did so with happiness and contentment. Then there were those who took their commitment to the ultimate level and became bonded mates, meshing their emotions as deeply as the man seated his cock inside his woman as the Sacred Vow was spoken. Forever entwined. One always a part of the other. Even beyond death.

That level of devotion was not something to take lightly, especially to a *Llanos* warrior who already was the ultimate example of responsibility and loyalty. *Jesu*, look what happened to Bale when his wife and child were killed. And they had only been married, for Bale hadn't trusted his wife enough to bond. The grief and guilt over being unable to protect them had annihilated the warrior's humanity, leaving him a seething cauldron of rage and vengeance that brought him all the way to Earth to kill Lucian, who he felt was responsible for the tragedy. Only Amaryllis' deft hand had brought Bale out of the well of suffering. Barely.

Amaryllis believed the warrior could be rehabilitated and Dhavin trusted his princess explicitly, but at times he wondered if perhaps Lucian had been right and the assassin should have been put down when the chance had arisen. Of course Amaryllis would have made earrings out of their testicles if they had succeeded.

If he were to lose Fiona, would he plunge into the abyss of despair like Bale?

No. No. That fate was not a possibility. While Earth had its share of hardships and strife, it was a paradise compared to the harshness of Skandavia. What a relief it was to know that in this little corner of the world, no war would harm them and there was no villain too ominous, for his powers would keep them safe.

The sensation of a sharp, razor-like sting under his right ear and a strangled cry brought him up short.

Over the pounding of his hearts, Dhavin listened through the wind. To the right, about a mile out, distress vibrated along the tree limbs like a tuning fork.

With the opening of the casino, the crime rate in town had steadily increased. A result that was to be expected when launching an industry that fed off lowered inhibitions and delusions of grandeur. Most of the misconduct was relegated to the casino itself or the streets leading to and fro. But the woods were lovely, dark and deep, or so he had once heard them described in a poem, and the thick, gnarly forest of the Cascade Mountain range concealed secrets of the illicit and nefarious kind.

The Deep South had their moonshiners, in the Northwest, it was meth labs. Score a small win in the casino and a celebratory dime bag was within easy reach. Short on funds? A pocket was readily available to pick.

Dhavin raced over frozen pine needles and crunchy leaves. Twenty yards from his destination he climbed up the sturdi-est-looking pine tree to perch in the foliage and observe the situation.

In the moonless night the players were nothing more than shadows moving through the darkness, but their heightened emotions were as effective as a spotlight.

Two men surrounded a third, who appeared bulky enough to be able to defend himself against his slighter-built opponents, but seemed to lack the will. He cried and held his hand to the side of his head as blood oozed from between his fingers.

"Shut up, bitch," said one of the assailants as he backhand-ed the howling man, knocking him to his knees. "Take your spanking like a good little girl."

"You didn't have to cut off my ear, dude," he whined in a high-pitched voice that sent a chill rattling along Dhavin's teeth like metal scraping metal.

"Why do you need it, if you don't listen?"

"I'm sorry, man. I said I was sorry. I'll have your money tomorrow. I promise." From his back pocket he withdrew a handful of tiny plastic baggies containing a spoonful of pow-der each. "Look, here's the stash Smithwick fronted me. Take it. It's all there."

Except for the ounce the man consumed earlier in the

evening, Dhavin noticed, digging his fingers into the tree bark as his vision blurred. Whatever strain of meth the man was on dulled his pain, but the adrenaline-laced panic feeding into his heart could not be controlled, pummeling Dhavin with the sensations. The man's drug-fueled terror scattered out in a dozen different directions, both cloudy and sharp, like shards of glass poking through cotton batting.

"It's not my money." Thug number one grabbed Earless by the hair. "Mr. Smithwick was very kind when he granted you an extension. Your directive was clear. Three new clients or ten Gs by Friday, otherwise your ass becomes ours to do with as we wish. My choice is to make Christmas decorations out of your body parts. Heinz here may have other uses for your ass. He has clients with some kinky tastes, but he'll have to try you out first."

Heinz, who up until now was a silent statue witnessing the proceedings, unclasped his hands to readjust his cock through his black slacks.

"No! Please don't fuck me. Let me go. I have two girls I can get you tonight. Let me call them and I can get them here in minutes, with cash. I'm telling you. They're ready to buy."

"If they were, you would have brought them to me already. And that still leaves you one short, Travis." He kicked Earless between the shoulder blades and stepped on his neck. "What do you say, Heinz? Want to teach this bitch a lesson?"

Dhavin pulled the cell phone from his belt and sent Reutgers, the deputy on duty, a text message.

The Chameleon's role was to be more of a deterrent than judge, jury and executioner, yet Dhavin wouldn't balk at eliminating a threat if needed. Only his respect of his sheriff and her judgment stayed his hand. The agreement Brett made with Kristos was that the Chameleon would never interfere with police business, and while the justice system of this world rarely dispensed true justice, Dhavin made the same promise when he agreed to bear the mantle. Permanently eliminating these undesirables required no effort on his part, however Brett would see the truth, and he did not want to disappoint his commander.

Reutgers replied seconds later with an affirmative and an ETA. Dhavin adjusted his stance, ready to make sure none of the party left the scene.

Smithwick was a name the police department was hearing more and more of in recent months. A player in the city, Smithwick had his fingers in larceny, drugs and prostitution. He sent associates to manage his projects, never leaving himself open to be identified. His poison was growing and beginning to infect scenic Cedar and endangering the quiet haven the citizens had taken pride in creating. Lucky for them, the Chameleon was there to beat crime's ugly head back into submission.

"Relax," Heinz rumbled in a voice made of gravel. He grabbed the back of Travis' baggy jeans and yanked them down, exposing the flesh of his ass. "You might like this."

"I think you'll like prison more," Dhavin called out, jumping from his perch and landing on graceful feet before the trio. Not even a drug dealer deserved to be desecrated in such a manner. "Make this easy on yourself and put your hands on your head."

Thug one was the first to wake from the shock of his arrival. "Hey, you're the lizard guy. Well, fuck you. We're conducting business here." He reached into the inside pocket of his jacket and pulled out a snub-nosed pistol.

"I see." Dhavin nodded his head. "Let me rephrase my request."

On an exhale he traced across the slight distance, grabbing the two hired guns by the lapels of their wool sports coats and knocking their skulls together before the cloud of his heated breath rose over his head. He dropped the bodies where they stood and cuffed their wrists with the plastic ties he kept in his satchel. He then strode over to the weeping Travis, who was rolling in the sticky pine needles, struggling in the dark to pull up his pants.

Dhavin waited for him to gather what shred of dignity he could muster. Once he was properly clothed, he stopped him with a firm shout. "Stay where you are. You will be going to jail. The choice is yours as to whether you go under your own control or slumped in a chair, like those two."

"Let me go, man. Please. Come on. I was almost ass-fucked."

"If you end up in the same cell as those two, you still might be. The night is young. Perhaps that will remind you what happens when you deal with nefarious people."

Travis picked up one of the plastic bags by his knees and held it up as if it were a winning lottery ticket. "Take them. Sell them, use it yourself. I don't care. Just let me go."

"What about Smithwick? Won't he be sending more men after you?"

"I don't care," he shrieked. "Just let me go."

Dhavin crouched down until they were nose to nose. "And how many others did you let go? How many did you keep from being destroyed by the drugs you provided them? How many lives did you help to their death?"

"Hey, man. That has nothing to do with me. I didn't put a gun to their head and force them to use. They came to me. If they want to fuck themselves up, that's their fault."

"What an appropriate choice of words. Considering you were about to be fucked yourself. As you said, that's your fault." He smiled and straightened to a stand as he sensed the careful approach of others. "Right on time, Officer Reutgers. Over here. All but one suspect is restrained, but I don't think he'll be giving you any trouble."

Reutgers and another officer stepped into the clearing with pistols at the ready. When they saw he had the scene secure, they lowered their weapons.

"You started without me?" Reutgers asked with a nod in greeting.

"Events were taking a turn for the gruesome and I could not, in good conscience, allow them to continue."

"What exactly do we got going on here?"

"For this one here, possession with an intent to distribute. As for those two, not much, unfortunately. They're Smithwick's men, but the most I can testify to is assault for the smaller of the two and attempted rape for the one he called Heinz."

"No! Don't say that!" Travis shouted. "Do you know what will happen to me if people hear that shit? Don't say anything, just keep them away from me."

Dhavin's powers picked up the slightest flicker of malice from the officer. Reutgers was as protective of his community as Brett was, and Dhavin sensed the idea of fucking with a person who threatened that safety was as alluring as a wallet full of dollar bills found on the sidewalk. No one would blame you for taking it, but that didn't make the deed right.

A cloud formed from Reutgers' mouth as he sighed and shook his head. "We'll leave the charges at assault. Nothing more. Thanks, Chameleon. We'll take it from here."

"Let me know if you require anything more from me."

"Got it." He scratched at the stubble on his chin. "How many of Smithwick's men have you roughed up now?"

Good question. He knew of eight he dealt with personally, but he had no idea of how many Kristos had put a stop to. "Not enough, in my opinion."

"Not that we don't appreciate the help, but you may want to call us in sooner. Stopping these thugs is our job, you're a private citizen. He may make things personal if you continue to interfere in his business."

"Don't worry about me, Officer. I'm more than capable of taking care of myself. Smithwick is but an annoying insect compared to the villains I've faced. If he wants to make it personal, I say have at me."

Reutgers shook his head. "You've got balls, Chameleon. I'll give you that."

"Do your part, Officer, and I'll do mine."

FIONA FELT HER stomach knot like pretzel dough as she and her aunt huddled around Mags while she scrolled through the weather forecast updates on her smartphone.

Snow, snow and more snow was expected to dump over half of the state beginning at eight that evening. How the meteorologists were so precise with their predications baffled her, but no matter what time the white stuff was expected to fall, the outcome was going to be the same—a crappy commute and lack of customers.

A dusting of snow was common in the wintertime with their location on the mountain but usually any precipitation melted by afternoon, disappearing as quickly as it arrived. This time however, the forecast was for feet of snow and below-freezing temperatures. On the steep, twisting mountain roads, that made a deadly combination.

Through the big picture window, the sun shone bright and beautiful, making it difficult to believe the storm of the century was on its way, but life on the mountain taught you to be prepared for anything. Two years earlier the town council downplayed weather reports less ominous than those currently playing and twelve people died when trying to navigate roads that should have been closed or treated for ice. Though the town's resources were slim, the lesson was learned and every precaution was taken to prevent another disaster.

The one upside of the impending doom was the shop was extra busy with people doing some last-minute shopping before becoming potentially homebound.

The bell chimed, announcing the arrival of two more customers.

"Good afternoon, Mrs. Dow," Fiona greeted the first guest while Bridget waited on the second and Mags continued to watch the trending topics on her phone. "What can I get for you today?"

"Chocolate. Chocolate. Chocolate," Mrs. Dow's four-year-old twins chanted, dancing a jig around the double-seated stroller carrying a toddler and baby girl.

"Cool it," their mother snapped then turned to Fiona with a sweet smile. "Yeah, like I need them hopped up on sugar before being trapped with them by the snow. Woo, what a day. The stores are crazy."

"So I've been hearing."

"Mitch called and the lumber mill told them to prepare to stay home tomorrow. Can you believe that? They never close."

Fiona's stomach soured more at that bit of news. When the

Cedar River flooded the year before and water breached the dam, the mill kept running. For them to be preparing for a closure meant they expected the weather to be really bad.

She wiped her damp hands against her pants. "Sounds like you'll have a full house."

"Yep. Can I have two dozen scones? If we're going to be trapped, I want my favorite foods on hand."

"Sure thing."

Mrs. Dow leaned closer to whisper, "And wrap up a cherry cake too. Mitch loves them and once the kids are asleep, we can share a treat and snuggle to keep warm. If you know what I mean."

Fiona looked at the twins shrieking as they chased one another around the table and then at the toddler affectionately picking his baby sister's nose and restrained a shudder. "How do you find the energy?" she asked before she could stop herself.

"My Mitch is a sexy man. Even more so when he's in dad-mode."

"More power to you, Mrs. Dow." Fiona had to admire her resilience. The woman was insane, but she was content with her reality, which was more than most people could say.

The bell chimed again and Fiona looked up to see Officer Kilsgaard dash through the doorway and press his body deep into the shadowy corner of the room. He stood statue still, and Fiona found herself holding her breath with him though she had no idea why. After several heartbeats four members of the

Cedar Women's Auxiliary Club crossed in front of the store. They paused by the door, looking around and gesturing in confusion. When Janice Harbinger met her gaze through the glass, Fiona gave a slight wave. The woman returned the gesture with halfhearted energy and shrugged, leading the rest of the club down the street.

Once their high-pitched chatter faded, Office Kilsgaard released a slow breath and stepped deeper into the room. "Good afternoon, all."

"Hey," Fiona replied. "Are you okay?"

"Fine. Fine. Hello, Mrs. Dow." He grabbed the twins by the back of the shirts as they flew past him. "Boys, make your mother proud and use your inside voices. Or else," he finished in a low tone.

The boys ran to their mother and grabbed on to each leg, staring up at the giant man with wide eyes.

"Thanks, Officer." Mrs. Dow laughed. "I think you may be the only person who can get them to be quiet. I may need to call you in the future."

"They're good lads, just young. Can I help you with your things?"

"No thanks. I've got a system." She tucked the parcel Fiona handed her into the bottom of the stroller and started for the door. "Thanks, Fiona. Good luck in the storm."

"Bye." Fiona waved, then felt the weight of Dhavin's gaze as silence fell between them.

With him standing before her in the flesh, guilt rolled in

her belly, which she knew was stupid. He didn't know she had intended to call him the night before, so there was no reason to feel as if she were unfaithful to him. Up until the moment she had dropped her keys, Dhavin had been on her mind. But that was before the Chameleon became Cam and a tiny tendril of hope that she would see the masked crusader again took root. A possibility. Again that word went and made everything complicated.

Was she envisioning a future of a long-term commitment and wedding bells? *Pfft.* Of course not. But she couldn't, in good conscience, entertain the notion of even flirting with the handsome policeman when her heart was pointing her toward another. One woman, one man. That was how she was programmed.

Nevertheless, heat spread across her cheeks as she remembered the fantasies she had allowed herself to spin about Officer Dhavin. In her imagination he was a playful kisser, teasing her lips with small nips of his teeth. Cam's kisses she imagined as more serious, deep and thorough, able to obliterate all other thoughts from her mind.

There was a brief moment before falling to sleep when she imagined both men stroking her from neck to toes and everywhere in between. Totally wicked and absolutely decadent.

And totally, utterly shameful.

"Fiona? You're flushed. What's wrong?" Officer Kilsgaard asked.

"Nothing." Except she was a horrible person. "It's been

busy and all this talk of the storm is freaking me out a little. I'm good, Officer."

"Please, call me Dhavin."

"You're working." And even if he weren't, he'd always be Officer Kilsgaard.

"I am. But I still want to be your friend, even though you turned me down. Maybe in time you will change your mind, however I may be waiting a long time for that after you see what I have for you. Hold out your hand."

From his jacket pocket he withdrew a small white envelope. It weighed perhaps an ounce, yet it felt like five pounds balanced on her open palm. "What is this?"

"Look inside."

The outside of the envelope was blank. Inside held a single sheet of paper. The blood rushed in her ears as she slid out the paper and saw the bold, blocked-lettered black script in the center.

Dessert?

7:30 your place. I'll bring the wine.

-C

Her brain refused to process the information. "I don't understand."

Officer Kilsgaard smiled. "You have an admirer."

"I still don't understand."

"This morning I responded to an accident near the Old Saw Bridge and," his voice lowered to a murmur, "our mutual acquaintance was there. He told me he had patrolled this area of town and asked me about you. Apparently you made quite an impression on him last night."

"I did?" she squeaked then flushed again when she noticed Aunt Bridget taking an avid interest in their conversation. She angled her body away from her too-interested aunt and asked in a more controlled voice, "You talked about me? What did he say? He really gave this to you?"

"Correct. And I am to report back to him with your answer. I've been instructed to ensure it is in the affirmative."

Had the world turned upside down? No way was she being asked out by the man of her dreams via the hunky guy she turned down the night before. This had to be a joke or else everything the officer said last night about his interest in her was a lie. "Why did you agree to deliver this? I mean, especially after yesterday."

He ran a finger over the smooth countertop, eyes downcast. "I like you, Fiona, and I want you to be happy. If not with me, then with someone else who deserves you. Believe me though, I'd rather you give me a chance. But the Cha—he's a good guy. And I think he's lonely. It's not like he has a lot of friends or someone he can relax around. You'll be good for him too."

Her fingers tightened on the paper that still carried the heat of Cam's touch, as if it were fresh from the copy machine. She drew the paper to her chest then realized tucking it between her cleavage was not the most mature move.

"Wow. I don't know what to say."

"Then I'll answer for you. I'll let him know you'll be waiting."

"How? Can't I call him?"

"He uses more elementary methods of communication. He has to be careful who has a direct line of contact to him. So is it a yes?"

The word came to her lips then clung to her tongue. Why was she suddenly afraid? It was only a meeting, after all. Not even a date. And here was this great guy standing before her, who made no bones about wanting to spend more time with her. What should she say? Who should she choose?

"Yes." The word came out on a breath.

One night. She could be reckless for one night.

The slow, sexy smile that curled his firm lips almost made her take the word back. Cripes, when did she go from having one potential suitor to two? Some women might think this was a good problem to have, but all Fiona wondered was what gods did she piss off to be tortured in this fashion.

"Good." He rapped his knuckles on the countertop. "If it doesn't work out between you two, will you reconsider my offer?"

She nodded. "Thank you, Officer…Dhavin."

"My pleasure. Bridget, love." He sauntered toward her aunt. "Is that a fresh batch of shortbread I smell?"

"Yes," her aunt answered slowly. Her narrowed-eyed gaze bounced back and forth between them. "This is the second day in a row you've been in. You must really like our sweets." She waggled her eyebrows at the innuendo.

"They are the best I've ever tasted. But you already know that." He winked. "Give me three dozen to take back to the station. Once that storm hits, it's going to be a long night for us on duty."

"Sure thing." She reached for a white box and began to load it with large handfuls, not even bothering to count. "This will be on the house."

"Auntie," Fiona exclaimed.

"All right, all right. Half price," she whispered.

Fiona let it go. After all, it was for a good cause and she had other things to worry about, like what to wear and what type of dessert would a superhero enjoy?

Warm *pot de crème* smothered over golden skin sounded absolutely decadent, but not for a first date.

Second date, maybe.

Chapter Four

TWENTY SECONDS.

Fiona rearranged the plate of tartlets on the table. The lemon chiboust filling was the perfect dessert for a first date. Not too heavy, refreshing and bright, plus the sweet-and-tart cream went well with either red or white wine. And nothing was flakier than her shortbread pie dough. She angled the dish so the light from the chandelier sparkled against the crystal, and looked at the clock on the wall again.

Only fifteen seconds more had passed? Gah!

Cam wasn't late. Not really. 7:32 did not count as late. Each tick of the second hand made it seem like an eternity, but her brain understood it was only nerves making her think she'd been waiting at the ready forever.

She grabbed a lock of hair and twisted the frizzy ends into some semblance of a curl and took another tour of the first floor. The carpet was freshly vacuumed, the junk mail had been tossed into the recycling and all the dishes were put away. One pair of shoes waited by the door, strategically arranged to look as if thrown without a care. She wanted to appear tidy but not unrealistically neat. It was best not to set too high of an example.

Maybe she should put the tartlets back into the refrigerator. No, too long in the cold and the tops could turn to rubber.
But if she kept them at room temperature any longer the
raspberry syrup drizzle might bleed into the cream, making an
unappetizing mess.

Refrigerate. Yes. No. Yes. Ugh.

A light rap on the sliding glass door drew her up short. For
several long seconds she stared at the venetian-blind-covered
window as her brain ceased to fire commands. A second knock
made her jump and she hurried across the room. Remember-
ing their conversation from the night before, she peeked
through the plastic slats instead of whipping open the door.
Cam rewarded her with a smile and an approving nod.

"Woo, it's cold," she couldn't help but shout after she slid
the glass open and a frigid breeze blew her hair back. White
flakes had begun to fall and dusted the ground like powdered
sugar. "Come on in."

She slid the door shut then looked up, way up and for the
first time in her life felt dainty.

Holy. Crap.

The Chameleon was standing in her dining room.

Yep, there went her cognitive ability. The house could be
burning down around them and she wouldn't notice, or even
care. His image blurred as her vision fuzzed out due to lack of
oxygen from her frozen lungs. That intense stare of his was a
laser beam to her core, sending a tingle of excitement zinging

through her bloodstream at the same time it scared her witless.

Dear Lord, please don't let me make an ass of myself.

"Thank you for accepting my invitation," he said as he withdrew a bottle of wine from the bag tied to his belt. "Especially since I invited myself over. No one knows where I live, and I need to keep it that way at least for now."

"Oh, I understand. Please, have a seat." She gestured to the chair at the head of the table. "Or would you prefer to sit in the living room?"

"The dining room is fine." He pointed to the plate. "Fiona, those look wonderful. I haven't seen tarts like this in your shop. Did you make these for me?"

Wait, he'd been *in* her shop? How did she not know this? She meant to ask, but his delighted smile distracted her. "I didn't know what you liked, so I went with a neutral flavor."

"I don't think you make anything I wouldn't like. I hope this wine goes well."

She took the offered bottle and snapped her teeth together to stop the girlish squeal that threatened to burst forth. "This is my favorite, and I can be picky with my wine. This will be perfect. Let me get us some glasses."

"Allow me."

He started to rise and she stopped him with a sharp, "No. You're a guest. Besides, when was the last time someone waited on you?"

"Longer than I can remember. I'm the type of man who usually does the serving."

"Not tonight. Sit. Relax. If you can."

His husky chuckle stroked her along the spine as she dashed into the kitchen and set a new world's record for uncorking a bottle of wine. She grabbed two of her finest crystal glasses and began to run back but forced herself to slow her steps. At the corner she paused to sneak a peek and admire him for a bit.

Man, he was impressive. Even seated, he was taller than she and his chest seemed to stretch as wide as the table. Perhaps it was her overactive imagination, but she swore little arcs of electricity sparked in a halo around him, as if his energy were protesting the stop of action.

"So," she began as she entered the room and poured a measure of red liquid into each glass. "How was your day? Ugh—no, don't answer that. It was a stupid question. Not that I don't care how your day was, 'cause I do, but that's just so lame. How was your day? How completely uninteresting on my part—"

"Fiona."

Her heart leapt into her throat when he placed his big, warm palm over her shaking hand and trapped her in the snare of his deep-brown gaze.

"Sit."

Her legs buckled and she plopped ungracefully into the chair that was fortunately positioned in the best spot to prevent her from falling on her ass.

"Breathe."

Her lungs expanded, immediately following his command.

"Good. Again." He nodded when she complied and smiled, which threatened her composure all over again. "I can feel your nervousness like I swallowed a live octopus. It's only me. Relax."

"I don't think I can."

"Why not?"

She felt her eyes boggle and gestured wide to indicate his grandness. "Because you're you. The Chameleon."

"I'm Cam. Just a man like any other."

She snorted, much to her horror. "Yeah, right. Doesn't matter. There are so many questions I want to ask you but don't know if I should, or if I even want to know the answers to them. I don't think I can have a normal conversation with you without coming off like a major dweeb and I...I..."

It hurt too much to look into those all-seeing eyes. Why couldn't she stop talking? With every word she spouted it was as if she was cementing her status as an uncouth goofball.

"Tell me, Fiona. Please." He recaptured her hand and gave her a reassuring squeeze.

"I want you to like me," she admitted in a small voice.

"I do like you. That's why I'm here."

No, like me, like me. Like me enough to throw me on the floor, smother me in lemon cream and lick me clean, like me, she wanted to shout. Instead she responded with a soft. "Oh."

"Ask me anything and I'll answer, if I can."

Her gaze immediately flew to the cowl covering his head

and face.

Will you take off your mask?

She bit her tongue and tried to force her mind onto another topic.

"You hesitate when I know there is something specific on your mind."

"No there isn't."

"Fiona. I will let you in on a secret only the sheriff knows about." He leaned closer. "I can sense emotions."

"Sense? Sense how?"

"When I told you I sensed your nervousness, I really can. Whatever emotion you are feeling, I feel too."

"All emotions?" she asked, though she knew the answer.

The corner of his mouth quirked up and his eyelids lowered. "All of them."

"This information does not put me at ease."

His chuckle slid over her like warm butterscotch. "I promise I won't hold anything I learn against you, even though you intrigue me beyond reason and I desperately want you to elaborate on some of what I've sensed going on inside you. In case it escaped your notice, I want you to like me too."

But she did. She liked him a lot. Probably more than he was ready for.

"Ask me," he encouraged with a whisper.

Dare she make such a bold request?

No.

He wore the mask for a reason and for all intents and purposes, they were still strangers to each other. Would the shape and planes of his face make a difference in how she felt about him? God, she hoped she wasn't so shallow.

What had she done thus far to warrant the trust needed to expose himself in such a fashion? Nothing. And she was going to prove that in her mind, he was more than a superhero.

"Where are you from?"

His eyes widened then narrowed, and for a moment she thought she had empathic powers and was able to taste his suspicion that she was hedging her own curiosity. He nodded once then answered, "How familiar are you with Saturn?"

"As in the planet? Wait. Are you an alien?" she shouted before she could temper the shock in her reaction.

"Yes, I guess that is what I am to you. I'm actually from the largest moon. You call it Titan, but to me it is Skandavia."

"You're serious, aren't you? Well, of course you are, but, seriously?"

Who knew aliens were so hot? No, she didn't mean to think that. But still. Who knew? He was certainly no little green Martian. Although Martians were from Mars and he was from Saturn, maybe that was the difference.

Why was she even debating this?

There was an honest-to-God alien sitting in her dining room, holding her hand! Since the Chameleon's first appearance, the townsfolk have been speculating about his origins. They all suspected he wasn't exactly human, but to know for certain he was an alien? From outer space? Pow! There went her mind, officially blown.

A strangled laugh choked her throat. "How? I mean—Wha—Why?"

"Breathe. Breathe, Fiona."

"I'm trying."

"I know it must be difficult to believe, but it's true."

"Why did you leave? Are you here on your own?"

The light in his eyes dimmed as he looked away and chewed on his bottom lip. Had she hit upon an off-limits topic already?

"No." He squeezed her hand. "Don't shy away. I haven't talked to anyone about my origins, and I didn't think it would be so difficult to do so."

"You don't have to tell me anything."

"I want to. I want you to know me." He drew in a breath. "This uniform I wear marks me as a guard for the royal family. Like with any nation, there was discontent and the king did not handle the rising conflict well. Not even the sage advice of our wisest council could sway him. I...was banished for failing to keep our queen safe when she risked meeting with the revolutionaries on her own."

"Earth was to be your prison?"

"Yes."

"And your powers? Do all people from your world have them?"

At this, he chuckled. "No. These abilities I have were unexpected. Except for the heightened empathy. It's so cold on

Skandavia we communicated by reading each other's emotions. But the strength, the speed, I never imagined, and believe me, it took me awhile to gain control."

"Did you have no one here to help you? No one to confide in?" She leaned forward, completely fascinated by his tale. An alien!

"With this?" He placed his palm over the center of his chest. "Too risky."

Then why me? The question blistered her tongue. She didn't let it free for she didn't want him to think about how unexciting she really was.

"Thank you for trusting me. I won't tell anyone anything."

"I know." His smile made her insides quiver. "How about a toast? To new friendships."

"That sounds nice." She clinked her glass to his and took a healthy swallow of the fruity wine.

"Now, tell me more about you—" he began and was cut off by a muted buzzing sound emitting from his belt. He withdrew a cell phone and frowned at the display before answering. "Ya?"

Interesting. There was a way to contact him without using the Cedar police force as a courier service. Fiona took another sip of wine and tried not to eavesdrop on the conversation. So what if the voice on the other end carried a distinctly high-pitched, female tone? If he wanted her to have his phone number, he'd let her know.

Dear Lord, he could sense her emotions! Patience, patience, she chided herself and focused on controlling the slight, miniscule, surge of jealously that shot through her heart. A needy, clingy woman would probably turn a man like him off.

Cam replied to whoever called with a series of one-word sentences and an occasional grunt before ending with, "I'll be there soon."

Disappointment squeezed her around the chest before she lassoed it tight and buried it deep inside her mind.

"You're getting stronger at doing that," he said as he slipped the phone back into his belt. "I almost didn't feel you at all."

She tried for her best doe-eyed innocent expression. "What do you mean?"

"I'm disappointed too." He ran the tip of his finger down her cheek and along the curve of her jaw and all the tension in her melted. "Don't be afraid to feel emotion around me."

"Some things I want to keep to myself. Besides, if you can sense my emotions, you can sense other's as well. I don't want to burden you."

"You will never be a burden, Fiona." He sighed and rose from his chair. "Obviously you know I have to leave. That was the sheriff. The snow is coming down fast and a logging truck has jackknifed at the bottom of 518 and is blocking most of the road. Traffic is light now, but it has to be moved before anyone crashes into it. Unfortunately Mac, the tow truck driver, has also slid off the road and is delayed."

She rose as well. "No. I understand. You have to help.

That's what you do. Can you wait one quick second?"

"Of course."

She hurried into the kitchen and tossed several brownies into a plastic bag then ran back to his side. "Take these for later. Who knows when you'll get a break."

He palmed the bag before placing it in his pouch. "Thank you. Can I see you again?"

"Yes, please."

He reached out and brushed the hair behind her ear, following the shell down to her neck, lightly skimming the sensitive flesh with the hot pads of his fingers.

All the air left her lungs and she swayed into his touch as pulses of electricity zipped along her skin, tightening her nipples and turning her thighs to jelly. God, those light touches were so addictive.

Cam gasped and his fingers tightened on her shoulder. "Ah, Fiona. You make it difficult to leave. I grieve over the night we could have had."

What? What did you have in mind and can it still happen?

She swallowed her tongue and tried for her most serene smile. "Good luck and be careful."

His hand fell away as he moved toward the door. An arctic chill swept through the house when he opened the door, yet it was the impending loneliness of him leaving that chilled her to the bone.

"I have to." She heard him mutter before he spun back around and cupped her face in his palms, stilling her for the descent of his mouth.

He kissed like he was built. Strong and hot, like the richest molten cocoa. The cold was banished as his big arms enveloped her in his heat and pressed her against the hard length of his body. His hips ground into the softness of her belly, making her whimper. Good gravy, was he hard.

This total loss of mind control was a novelty. Who knew that one smoldering kiss could sap all her strength, leaving her unable to do anything but hang like damp cheesecloth?

Just as she was about to pass out from the lack of air, he let her go, catching her arm as she stumbled.

"Tomorrow? Same time?" he panted.

"Ah, um." She nodded, her throbbing lips refused to work.

Before she could blink, he was gone, only the path of his quick footsteps in the already deep snow indicated his direction.

Her hands shook as she closed the door. Pressing her head against the cold glass, she enjoyed the cooling sensation on her skin before she jerked back with a gasp.

Tomorrow? He wanted to see her tomorrow.

How much of her did he want to see?

She raced to the bedroom and dove into her underwear drawer, searching for the sexy pair of black lacy panties Aunt Bridget gave her for a joke to wear when she dragged her to see the Chippendales the year before.

"Oh shoot. Razor." She dashed into the bathroom and rummaged through the cabinet, shouting in triumph when she found her last new razor cartridge.

It didn't hurt to be prepared. And if Cam was interested in sampling her confections, she was going to make sure the presentation was perfect.

Chapter Five

SNOWMAGEDDEN WAS THE name the news anchors gave the storm that raged outside. Three feet of snow and ice had fallen overnight, covering half of the state and creating panic all over the entire Northwest. In some places it piled five to six feet deep. Needless to say, Fiona never made the drive into work.

Along with the heavy snowpack, the wind was barreling down the mountain at speeds of up to sixty miles an hour. Between cars sliding off the road and tree branches coming down like rain, the news had been broadcasting nonstop and the police had been going just as hard.

It had taken her thirty minutes to clear a path to the stock-pile of firewood near the shed and another ten to get a blaze rolling in the wood-burning stove. If it was possible to sit on the metal hearth to get the feeling back into her frozen limbs, she would have jumped on bare-assed naked.

There was a reason why she hadn't followed her parents when they moved to Buffalo, New York, and harsh winters was it. When the weather turned sour, they quickly relocated to Arizona, but by then she had opened up the shop and was content to stay put.

The power went out as Fiona watched the noon news telecast with a pillow clutched tight to her chest. She never realized how silent silence was until the hum of the refrigerator and the buzz from a bright light bulb was suddenly cut off like a meat cleaver through a power cord. Alone in her house with the wind howling outside, she felt as if she were left all alone on the planet.

While her little house was not out in the sticks, she wasn't close to town either. It could be hours before power was restored, but her gut told her it was probably going to be a day, if not more. She paced a circle around the living room and pulled at the ends of her hair. By her feet sat a stack of books. Not one of them interested her enough to go beyond page one. Sitting and waiting was not her style. Relaxation was a scheduled event, usually occurring after a hard day's work.

How could she pretend that the day was a holiday when people were in danger? Aunt Bridget was alone, Mags had texted her saying the pipes in her rental house burst and Cam was probably out protecting the town.

She pressed her nose against the sliding glass door and worried her lip. The sky was a deep, dark slate, making day appear almost nighttime. Cam's footprints from the night before had long since been obscured with the continual snowfall. The glass fogged over with her breath and she wiped the spot clear with her sleeve then frowned as she caught sight of movement in the distance. From the vast expanse of white and gray a figure emerged, trudging slowly through the snow. Had a wild animal gotten lost and was looking for shelter? Perhaps it was a motorist who had crashed and needed help?

The motorist was a more dangerous creature, in her opinion. There was being charitable and then there was allowing a mass murderer into the house. Of course, what would a mass murderer be doing out in the middle of a snowstorm? Didn't matter. A stranger was a stranger.

Speaking of strange, the figure was huge, with a large hump on its back. Its torso disappeared, making it look like a floating head. A second later, the image was whole again.

"Cam," she breathed and opened the door to shout, "Cam."

He lifted a hand and hurried his steps.

"Why are you letting the cold air in? You'll freeze," he said as he neared. Once inside, he shut the door and pulled the drapery closed. "Do you have a towel? I don't want to track water everywhere."

"Yeah. One second." She ran to the bathroom for the cloth. "Is everything all right? Why are you here? Not that I'm sorry you're here."

"Thank you." He nodded and took the towels from her. He had toed off his boots and socks, which made her smile. Of course he'd have big feet. Large, strong, gnarly man-feet with scars and bumps. The feet of a soldier. "How are you faring?"

"Fine, all things considered. I have heat. That's more than some."

"True. True. Even I'm finding the cold too much to bear."

"Well, come closer to the fire. How long have you been out?"

"Most of the night." He blotted at the snow covering his head and shoulders. "One accident turned into two, then ten, then when the wind picked up, the trees began to come down. I've never seen trees explode in such a fashion before. The willow tree in the middle of the square split right down the middle. The trunk splintered like toothpicks."

"Oh no. I love that tree. It's been there since time began."

"Unfortunately, it's one of the many causalities of this storm. I'm afraid once this snow has cleared, Cedar won't appear as it once was. Your shop is fine, but the roof collapsed on the shops on the other side of the street, and I've lost count of the number of homes that have been damaged."

"Has anyone been hurt?"

"Physically? Nothing that won't heal in a day. Emotionally? Well, only time will tell."

"God, I hate snow." She gestured to the pot of water bubbling on the stove. "Would you like some coffee? How about soup? I can feed you something hot."

"Coffee sounds wonderful." He settled back into his chair with a chuckle. "Look at you. French press. Heavy skillets. You're a regular pioneer woman. Ready for anything."

"I know wood-burning stoves are considered retro now, but the power goes out at least once a year and with a regular fireplace you have to sit in the hearth to feel any heat. I'll take a good ole potbellied monster anytime."

"The Anderson's home was blazing bright when I passed by there earlier. I heard part of their remodel included two generators."

"You know a lot for a person who lives in the shadows."

"The shadows keep the best secrets."

What she wouldn't give to learn what he did in the shadows. "I've thought about getting a generator, but then part of me thinks I'm just asking to lose power if I do. How do you take your coffee?"

"Slightly sweetened." He took the offered mug and sniffed appreciatively. "This smells fantastic. We don't have sugar where I'm from and it's now my favorite food group."

"No sugar? You mean you didn't have desserts or candy? I can't imagine a world without sweets."

"We had confections, but nothing like here. If you brought your talents to my planet, you would be worshipped like a goddess."

Heat from his smile warmed her cheeks. "You liked my brownies?"

"Loved them. I made the mistake of sharing them with the officers I was working with last night and almost didn't get one. You have many fans."

His compliment filled her with pride like no other she'd ever received. Why was that? Was it because she valued his opinion more than others, or was it pure attraction that made her want to lay her head in his lap like a puppy and beg for more attention?

Outside the pop and crackle of tree limbs bursting and crashing to the ground quieted and the hush rolled into the house. Unable to remain still, she reached for the poker and opened the front hatch to prod at the blazing logs.

"So." She licked her lips. "When is the sheriff expecting you back? Hopefully you'll get the chance to rest."

"I've been instructed to not show my face for a while. Besides, I don't think there will be a soul outside now that the sun is setting. It will be too foolish. My time is my own, for now."

"Oh."

She turned away to prevent him from seeing the delighted grin stretching her lips from ear to ear.

Crap, he probably sensed the zing of excitement that shot through her. *Relax. Relax. Relax. Do not think about Cam and you. Alone. In a blizzard.*

Hysterical laughter tickled her throat, threatening her attempt at appearing blasé.

"What's so funny?"

Damn. This empathy thing was maddening. "Nothing."

"Tell me. Your humor feels like bubbles against my skin. What is it?"

"It was nothing, really. Just a silly cliché."

"I don't not know this word, cliché. What does it mean?"

"Well, it's a phrase or idea that has been overused so when it's spoken, everyone can finish your sentence for you."

He leaned forward in his chair and rubbed his hands to-gether. "Now I am curious. What was this cliché?"

"It was stupid." As she talked she felt her cheeks burn as if she set them directly on the hot hearth. "Just. You know. Here we are. A girl and a boy." Boy. She mentally snorted. Ha! "Trapped in a storm. Whatever shall we do?" she finished in a singsong voice.

"Hmm." He stroked his chin. "I know I'd like to have sex with you."

The poker dropped from her hand and bounced as it hit the carpet with the same boy-oy-oying sound that echoed inside her skull. White dots floated in her vision and from a distance she barely heard his sharp command.

"Breathe, Fiona. Breathe."

Like a goldfish flopping next to its bowl, she sucked in a mouthful of air and warbled out a weak, "What?"

"I am certain you heard me."

"But—uh. Why?"

He rose to his feet and stalked toward her with slow, lazy steps. "Ah, Fiona. I heard you were a woman who liked a man who was direct. I thought it was because you are a person who likes to get right to the point, but now I realize it's because you don't believe what is right before your eyes."

"And what is that?"

The flames in his eyes glowed brighter than the candles surrounding them. The pads of his thumbs ghosted across her lower lip as he cupped her face. "A man who wants you so desperately, I swear I can already taste the salt of your skin on my tongue."

Yeaaahhh. That's so hot.

His lips settled on hers in a kiss that was as a far cry from the hastiness of the night before. He supped on her mouth as if she were a fine brandy, savoring her flavor. He cradled her in his arms as if he had all the time in the world and intended to enjoy her for every one of those seconds.

She let out a surprised gasp as her back met the wall, so lost was she in his kiss she didn't realize they had moved. Before her next breath, her shirt was up and over her head and her cotton-covered breasts were cupped in his hands. Chills raced down her arms as he peppered the exposed tops with biting kisses. Between the fireplace and his heated touch, a fine layer of sweat began to bead on her skin.

He buried his face in her cleavage and inhaled deep. "*Jesu*, you are so soft. Like a marshmallow."

The sentiment was sweet, but not exactly sexy. She pulled in her stomach and held her breath, fighting to regain the confidence she had only a moment before.

"The fire of your desire has dimmed." He pulled away and brushed the loose strands of her hair off her cheeks. "What are you thinking in that pretty head? The truth."

"I," she croaked then cleared her throat. "I want you to find me perfect."

"Silly girl." He kissed her cheek. "You are perfect. No, wait."

A sharp tug ripped the front of her bra open, the shredded fabric fell to the floor without a further thought. He pulled the band from her hair and fanned the tresses over her trembling breasts.

"Now you're perfect." He twisted a straining peak with his fingers. "You have no idea how long I've dreamt about seeing you this way. Naked and wanting me. Eager for my touch."

"Really?" He had? "How long?"

He laughed. "Since the moment I saw you."

Whatever thought she was about to have next was obliterated when his lips sealed over hers and the tug at her nipple strengthened. The sequin-like roughness of his tunic scraped her other sensitive peak and made her thighs clench as an ache formed between her legs. She ground against the hard length of his thigh, uncaring if the gyrations said, *I'm a slut, take me now.*

Cam stepped back, his chest heaving. "Now I'm the one who needs to remember to breathe."

He uncoiled the belt around his waist and pulled the tunic over his head. To her surprise, the cowl was attached to another half-shirt that stretched across his shoulders and formed the sleeves encasing his arms. The wide expanse of his heavily muscled chest was left gloriously bare. Soft brown hair ran down his belly and disappeared into black pants that molded to his legs, emphasizing the weighty bulge that strained the fabric and made her hands itch to wrap around his hot cock and squeeze.

"That's my *konkattie*. Later, I promise you can do all the things I can feel in your gaze, but first I need a taste of your nectar."

Did he say what she thought he said?

He dropped to his knees and tugged her jeans and panties down her legs in one pull. He nudged her thighs apart and touched the tip of his tongue to the top of her slit.

"Whoa!" She jerked back as far as the wall behind her allowed and grasped the sides of his face. "No, you don't have to."

"Don't have to what?"

"You know. This." Oh God, could her face flame any hotter with embarrassment? "You *know*. You don't have to do something you don't want because you think it might make me happy."

If she could see his eyebrows, she was certain they had jumped to his hairline. "You don't like having oral sex performed on you?"

Geez, she always thought she was mature when it came to sex, but Cam made her feel like a doddering virgin. "I do, but men don't."

He snorted. "This man does. Believe me, this is for my pleasure as much as it is yours. I'll have to do a proper job of convincing you. Part your legs for me. I know you're wet. Let me see."

Ah, no way. She was not the *spread my legs, see what I got* type of girl. Lights off, covers up to the chin, have sex by braille was more her style.

Of course, in the dark she wouldn't be able to see the glaze of unadulterated lust blazing in his eyes as he urged her thighs farther apart and ran the edge of his thumb along her slick folds, or watch with bated breath as he licked his lips before placing an open-mouthed kiss directly onto her clitoris.

Her knees buckled, but he was there to catch her, hooking her leg over his shoulder to feast on her pussy at his leisure. With nowhere to place her hands, they fell onto his head, her fingers digging into the smooth fabric of his cowl. Under the hood his hair was thick in her grasp.

The notion that he actually had hair on his head made her want to giggle, but then his teeth nipped at her swollen bud and the chuckle turned into a moan. Her fingers clenched and unclenched against his scalp as she struggled with the decision to pull him away or yank him closer to grind against his mouth. The ache gathering in her core was unbearable. Or at least she thought it was until he sank three fingers into her sheath.

"Motherfucker!" The expletive burst out in a very unlady-like fashion as her body bent double. "Cam. It's too much."

"There can never be too much pleasure. I can do this for hours. *Jesu*, you taste so good." He started a suction-lick-suction rhythm that brought tears to her eyes. The vibrations of his moans traveled from clit to nipples and added to the frenzy of electricity that blinded her to everything but Cam and his touch.

Okay. She believed him. Cam didn't like oral sex. He loved it. He devoured her as if she were a pie in a contest and the winner received an explosive orgasm.

Her climax was close, so close she felt the flames of the supernova lapping at her conscience. One. More. Second.

"Not yet." Cam lowered her leg and stood.

"What?" she panted. "No. Don't stop. Please, oh, please."

"I'm not stopping. Just pausing." His amused chuckle set her teeth on edge.

"If you leave me like this I will hate you forever."

"Well, we can't have that now, can we?" He reached for the bag on his belt and pulled out a roll of condoms. "Trust me, I have no intention of stopping."

"Thank you, Lord," she mumbled. Praise be to the man who comes prepared.

The foil wrapper fluttered to the floor and he loosened the drawstring of his pants, unleashing the heavy length of his cock.

And there went the last of her strength. The two partners that consisted of her list of previous lovers wouldn't have been considered small in the penis department by any means, but in no way did they measure up to Cam. It was ridiculous to call a man's cock beautiful, but Cam's was. Marble statue-Norse god stuff of legends.

Of course, that could be the hormones talking. At this point she was so horny, she didn't care what size he was, as long as he plowed it inside her. Now.

"You undo me, *konkattie*." He rolled the condom over the twitching shaft. "With only your gaze on me I could come."

"Bedroom is that way," she said, however she lacked the coordination to point, or even gesture in the right direction.

"Too far." He scooped her up and hooked both legs over his strong forearms. "This will do."

Her mouth fell open with each inch he pressed inside her. Man, and she thought his fingers were thick. The burn was sweet and delicious. Like dipping her finger into too-hot caramel. The slide as he pulled back out was just as maddening as her sheath tightened, unwilling to let him go. Before she could catch her breath, he punched his hips forward, sending him deep into her core then pulled back to lunge again. She buried her face against his neck and bit back a shout, hanging on for dear life as he set the pace of the wildest ride she'd ever been on.

The wall at her back shook as he thrust fast and deep, the pictures of Edinburgh Castle and the Piazza di Scala on either side of her head swung on their hooks and rattled with the motion.

She hung, suspended in his hands, and rode the terrifying edge to sweet oblivion. She felt as if she were on a swing, flying higher and higher into the air and the only way off was to jump. While the ride was exhilarating, she knew eventually she was going to have to come down, and the leap would be just as thrilling. But the landing was what frightened her most. A crash from that high was going to smash her to pieces. What type of women would she be once she became whole again?

Cam shifted, moving his hands from her backside to the wall and swiveled his hips, grinding the base of his cock against her throbbing clit. This time she screamed and bit into his shoulder.

"That's my girl. Come with me." His hotly panted words washed over her ear. "I'm going to come inside you. When I do, you will be mine. Do you understand?"

Yeah. Sure. Whatever. Just make the ache go away.

"Fiona," he groaned. "Do you understand?"

She nodded and swallowed another scream as lights burst behind her tightly closed eyelids and a fireball exploded deep in her core. The strength in her arms and legs gave out, and she melted in his hold, completely supported by the press of his hips wedged between her thighs.

Was it Cam or a product of his species that enabled her to feel the hardening of his cock as he jetted hard in her channel, the flex and twitch stroked hidden nerve endings that drew out her climax until her head swam?

"You," he started then stopped to lick at his dry lips. "Amazing."

He pressed his cowl-covered forehead against her sweaty brow. "You were holding out on me. Every moan, every scream. I want to hear them. Don't shy away from me again."

Again? He wanted to do this again?

Holy hell. Her inner muscles clenched around his still-hard shaft at the thought. No way was she going to survive another orgasm like that, no matter how sensational the ride.

"Which way to the bedroom?"

She nodded in the appropriate direction, still unable to co-ordinate her limbs properly to even point.

"Excellent." He placed a biting kiss on her shoulder. "I'm still hungry and this time I want to eat my meal in bed."

Tremors shook her body as a picture of her obituary flashed in her mind.

Fiona Corrione passed away at the age of thirty-one due to a case of out-of-this world orgasms. She was found in her home, naked, drenched with sweat and man fluids with a permanent smile stretching her lips.

Aunt Bridget would be proud.

✦　✦　✦

DHAVIN CURSED THE cowl covering his head as he tugged the soft, warm, sleeping woman closer to his side. How could he fully enjoy the lushness of her breasts with a layer of fabric between his cheek and her skin?

He wanted her fingers pulling at his hair and the sweet cream of her pussy coating his face. He wanted to speak to her with his own voice, and not the throat-scraping fake accent he used as the Chameleon. He wanted her to look him in the eye and scream *his* name as her sheath milked his cock. There was so much passion inside Fiona that she hid behind uncertainty. The glimpse he saw of her this afternoon only whetted his appetite to see her without any reservations.

For a human, she had an amazing ability to obscure her emotions. She concealed them in a sheer veil, hinting at but never broadcasting how she felt, leaving him to second-guess his plan of action.

In truth, he could not blame her. As long as the mask was between them, he could not expect her to be completely honest with her emotions. He hated lying to her, even though it was a necessity at this stage of their relationship.

If it was only his life in the equation, he'd risk telling Fiona everything, but there was his family to consider. Once he was secure with his place in her life, then all would be revealed. She was a smart girl. She'd understand the need for secrecy.

Until then, he was going to make the most of their seclusion and learn more about his *konkattie*. For instance, what type of sound would she make if he sucked hard at her dusky-pink nipple?

He slid his hand up her curved stomach and cupped a palm full of breast, scraping his nail over the silky peak. When the tip beaded, he switched to the other side and sealed his lips over the bud with a greedy suck.

A low, throaty groan eased past her lips and vibrated down her chest to buzz against his lips. He smiled and drew the flesh deeper into his mouth.

She pressed her torso closer, her hands rising to his head and her fingers searching for purchase. Again he cursed the cowl covering his face.

"Cam," she moaned. "Is that you?"

He had to laugh at that. "I hope so. Were you expecting someone else?"

"No." She arched with a gasp as he nipped at her second breast and laved the hurt with his tongue. "It's so dark in here, I can't see squat. I was afraid I had dreamt the afternoon and it was all in my imagination."

"Thankfully, my love, this is real. But you're right. It is too dark in here." Before she moved to prop up on one elbow, he had retrieved two candles from the living room and lit the wicks.

"Oh my God." She sat up with a start. "I forgot about the candles. I could have burned the house down."

"Rest easy. I put them out after you fell asleep."

She slapped her hand over her eyes. "Thank you. That would have been horrible."

"Do not fret. It was my fault you weren't thinking about potential fire danger. If I left you with rational thought, then I didn't make love to you properly." He slipped back under the covers and pulled her into the curve of his body. His left hand returned to plucking at her nipple. "Where was I? Ah, yes, enjoying your breasts, but now I can see you."

"Oh, right." She stiffened in his arms and the flare of her passion dimmed. She cleared her throat and burrowed closer against his side. "Your skin is so warm. I must feel like a popsicle in comparison."

"Not exactly. You're warm where it counts. Like here." He pressed his palm over her heart. "And here." He bent to her lips and thrust his tongue into the wet cavern of her mouth. "And here." He ran his finger under the plump curve of her breast before skimming down her belly. "And my personal favorite."

"Cam," she groaned as he pressed two fingers into her slick sheath.

Her greedy little hole sucked on his digits as he pressed the heel of his hand into her mound. "I am sensing discomfort. Are you all right?"

"A little sore." She shifted her hips, allowing his fingers to probe deeper. "I've been using muscles that haven't seen action in a long time."

"While part of me is pleased to hear that, my head cannot fathom why you are not mated already."

"Mated," she repeated with a delicate snort. "I'm picky. Haven't found the right guy yet."

"I am pleased that you found me worthy. I thank you."

The cutest shade of red stole over her cheeks. "No problem. Ah, that feels so good."

Even as her pussy melted in his hand, and her breathing grew labored, a beam of tension ran through her center.

"Um." She nibbled on her lip. "What about you? Have you been with many Earth-women?"

Now? She wanted to discuss his sex life now? No, no, no, no.

"I do not, how do you say, kiss and tell? Besides, none of them made me feel like you do."

"Them?"

This line of questioning had to stop. He kissed her hard, adding a third finger into her cunt and rubbing the soft spot high inside. He swallowed her whimpers and thumbed her tightly beaded clit until she softened into the mattress. When he was confident she could not form a sentence, he leaned down to suckle at her breast.

From half-lowered lids, he watched her expression as he felt the rise of her impending orgasm. Sweat dotted her forehead and her lips bowed as she panted. Her eyes were squeezed tightly shut. He recalled she had done the same thing the previous times they made love. Even when he was balls-deep inside her and his breath fanned her cheek, her eyes were closed.

"Open your eyes, Fiona."

"That's okay. I'm good."

Curious. "I want to see how dark they get when I make you come."

Little spasms rolled in her sheath. "Um, I can concentrate better if they're closed."

"Fiona." He nipped at her breast when she refused to respond. "Fiona. Look at me."

"I don't want to."

"Please explain."

A stuttering breath filled her lungs. "If my eyes are closed, then I can pretend you're not watching me."

"But I am watching you."

"I don't need to know that," she groused, and tried to curl her body into a defensive shell.

"Explain your words and open your eyes, please."

In response she reached for his cock, sliding her fingers down the length and cupping his balls. "I want to touch you."

Wicked girl didn't play fair. "Later. Why won't you look at me?"

"I am looking at you."

"Staring at my cock doesn't count." He pinned her roving hands to the pillow. "If you don't look at me, I won't touch you for a week."

That worked. "That's just cruel." The dark irises flickered between heat and frustration.

"Tell me what is going on in that complicated head of yours."

"It's stupid. Just forget everything about the last five minutes."

With the heat of desire ebbing, his senses picked up what she refused to speak. In his belly her insecurity made his insides pitch as if he were riding in a small boat in a choppy sea where mentally you knew you were safe, but the fear of being tossed overboard refused to leave.

In this she reminded him of Amaryllis when he first became her guard. After years of being told she wasn't good enough, she began to believe the lies brought on by other's jealousy and own self issues. Only when he showed her the beauty of her body and spirit did she embrace the powers that came with being an intelligent, confident woman. It appeared Fiona needed the same lessons, however this time, it was not with the intent, as with Amaryllis, that she find another to share her life with, but to accept a life with him.

"Why would I want to forget any of my time with you?" He brushed a soft kiss across her lips. "Do you know what I see?"

"Me," she said in a small voice.

"No. I see the part of you you don't believe exists. One look from you and my hearts squeeze. The curve of your smile brings tears to my eyes. And your curves. *Jesu*, I want to fill my hands with your flesh." And he did, cupping her hips and burying his face between her breasts. "I want to gorge on you, feast until I burst on the sweetness that is you."

Under his hands she trembled with her vulnerability, her breath stuttered in hot puffs.

"Watch me, Fiona. See what touching you does to me."

With his lips and hands, he stroked over the fleshiest parts of her body, attempting to show her how much he enjoyed the softness that was Fiona. When her eyes threatened to close, he bit or pinched her back to attention.

He slid his fingers back into her sheath and cursed at the slickness he found. Ah, to fell such wonder around his bare cock would be heaven beyond imagine. A lesser man might have given in to the temptation and seek his own gratification, but this moment was for Fiona.

"That's right, *alskata*, look at me." He thumbed her clit

and massaged the tightening walls. "Give your cries to me."

"Cam." She reached down and grasped his wrist, pressing his hand harder against her flesh. "Don't stop. If you stop, I'll kill you."

He laughed. "Then don't look away. Let me see you. Give me what I want, and I'll give you what want."

Those dark eyes speared him through the hearts. Need and desperation in the brown depths reminded him of the inside of a molten chocolate cake. Her nails dug into his wrist as her pussy clamped tight and she cried out his name. Her orgasm washed over him, tugging at his balls to join her in oblivion, but he clenched his teeth against the urge. She got what she wanted, now it was his turn.

When the spasms subsided and she fell back against the pillows in a panting heap, he withdrew his hands and coated his aching cock with her sticky honey. The tip throbbed a deep purple and wept with his pent-up seed.

"Cup your breasts for me." The huskiness of his command sounded foreign in his ears.

Her hands shook as she took the plump mounds in her hands. Swinging a leg over her torso, he nestled his slick cock against her sternum and pressed her breasts together to hug the shaft.

As he watched the dark-pink length glide in and out of her cleavage, the fire of his impending orgasm twisted low in his spine.

"Do you know," he stopped to catch his breath, "how

many...times I've imagined...spraying your breasts with my cum?"

The pleasure she felt at hearing his words caressed him as firmly as if she ran her hand down his back.

Her smile widened and she lifted her head to swipe her tongue at his crown bumping against her chin.

"Yes, yes, yes, yes," he chanted. "Open your mouth."

With a siren's smile she complied, allowing him to feed her his length and bathe him with her tongue. When he was good and wet he pulled out and resumed fucking her cleavage. He slipped back to her mouth when the rubbing became uncomfortable.

Her hands roamed over his skin, stroking everywhere she could reach. Her nails scored down his sides and across his buttocks, encouraging him to use her at his will.

"I'm going to come," he warned when the pressure reached a boil. "Where do want it?"

"Everywhere." She flicked out her tongue as an enticing target.

"Mother take me," he groaned and emptied his shaft into her waiting mouth. The satisfaction of watching his cum jet over her lips and splash onto her breast lengthened the release.

Helpless to resist, he melted, collapsing next to her on the bed. His breaths wheezed in and out as if he'd just scaled Mt. Rosenorn in record time.

Fiona skimmed her hands over her rosy breasts. She collected a dollop of his semen on her finger and looked at it with curiosity curving her brow.

Was she? No. How can she be?

Hurt filled his chest, but he had to ask. "Did I disappoint you?"

"What?" Her genuine surprise eased some of the wound. "No. That was the most erotic moment of my life. It was mind-blowing."

"Please tell me what you are thinking."

The pink of her cheeks deepened. "Your cum, it's salty and white. Like an earthling."

"Is that bad?"

"No. I just thought it might glow in the dark, or something like that. But no. You're normal."

The exuberance of his laugher caught him off guard and made him cough as it burst from his lungs. Normal? What did he have to do to impress his woman?

"Ah, Fiona. You are like no other I have ever met. In this world or another."

"What does that mean?"

He cuddled her close. "It means you are perfect, in every way."

Chapter Six

FIONA CRADLED THE hot ceramic mug closer to her chest and stared out the window at the destruction that was her backyard. After three days of snow, the wind had picked up and sheared off all the branches of almost every tree in the neighborhood. During the night she and Cam had sat in silence and watched the fireworks show of transformers exploding in blue-green flashes across the mountain. With every snap, crackle and crash that sounded like gunfire, she had burrowed deeper into his arms, but not even his strength made her feel safe from the threat of a falling tree. In the light of day she counted five tree limbs as thick as her thigh embedded into the ground like javelins thrown by the gods during a track and field event.

Her cell phone had long ago lost power, and the loss of contact to anyone outside her home put her on edge. As much as she hated to be alone for any length of time, she didn't balk when Cam said he needed to go out and see if his services were needed. Far be it for her to be selfish and keep him all to herself. In a show of support she had packed him with enough food for two days and a plea to check on her aunt. His goodbye kiss promised she would be rewarded for her understanding.

A smile stretched her lips as her aching body began to tingle. Dear Lord was she sore, but the burn was oh so worth it. Sex with Cam had to be the best exercise in the universe. She'd make it a point to work out every day, if she had a routine like that.

Every day.

There was that word again. Every. It made her think of the future and what would happen once the roads cleared. What was going on with her and Cam? Were they dating? Was this just a fling brought on by extreme circumstances?

A dull throb took residence in her frontal lobe. She didn't want to think about it. Obviously this fairytale time had to come to an end, but she'd enjoy the moments as they came, no matter if the insecurity of tomorrow killed her.

The sky was growing dark and she wondered if Cam planned on coming back to her that night. If he was needed to help others, of course he should continue his work, but a note would be nice if he had a means to relay the message. As it was, she didn't think sleep was in the cards for her that evening, especially without his protective embrace.

Her heart leapt as she saw him emerge from the tree line and run in her direction. She opened the sliding glass door before he reached out a hand. "You came back?"

"Of course I did." He stomped on the mat to clear his boots of snow. "Silly girl, I'm not leaving you alone in this weather. And without a proper goodbye. I have good news. The forecast calls for rain later this evening and overnight temperatures in the forties. All of this white stuff will be a distant memory by tomorrow morning."

Morning. There it was. The death toll on the fantasy. She forced a smile as she said, "That's great. Did you find out anything about my aunt?"

He tapped her on the end of her nose. "I'm disappointed too."

Damn. She had to get better at hiding her emotions. "My aunt."

"I found her at Mr. Hendrix's. He has a generator and the entire block is camping out at his house. They were playing gin rummy, but without the cards."

"Good. At least she's safe."

He grunted an agreement. "There are at least ten houses in town with tree damage. We're lucky."

"We are. I hope you were able to help."

"As best as I could." He held up the pack he had strapped to his chest. "I've brought a few supplies."

He drew out a bottle of wine, ten caramel chocolate bars and a giant box of condoms.

"Do I want to know how you acquired these?"

"Downtown has power and some of the shops have reo-pened."

"You walked in and bought these? Dressed like that?"

He laughed at her shocked expression. "Of course not

dressed like this. Word of The Chameleon loading up on liquor and condoms would spread faster than a wildfire."

She waited for him to elaborate, but he remained silent as he kicked off his boots and made himself at home. He must have a disguise then of some kind. What could it be? Had she seen him in it and not even known?

"What are you wearing?" The sharp, disapproving tone in his question startled her out of her train of thought.

The velour pants and sweater that had been so comfortable not a moment before felt constricting around her thighs and waist. "It's a track suit."

He shook his head and folded his big arms across his chest. "What are the rules about clothes?"

Heat raced up her neck and scalded her cheeks. Her thighs clenched and her nipples hardened at his reminder. After their first night together, Cam had declared a no-clothing rule for the rest of the storm. He claimed it was so she would feel more comfortable in her skin. She thought it was because he wanted easy access to her body whenever he wanted. Not that she had that big of an issue with his request. At least not after she caught him staring at her as if she were a juicy steak and he had been forced to live on a diet of twigs and grass for too long.

Despite his encouragement, she still wasn't comfortable walking around totally bare. Thank God the power was still out and she had the blessing of soft candlelight to hide the worst of her flaws.

"I was cold, and you weren't here." She fiddled with the edge of her sweatshirt.

"I'm here now." He reached for his belt. The rustle of cloth hitting carpet made her thighs tense. The tunic was next to go, leaving him gloriously bare-chested "Strip."

The force in the word stroked along her back like the tail end of a whip. Her hands shook as she pulled the tab of the zipper down and exposed her breasts. By the way his smile curled, she knew he liked that she was braless beneath the soft fabric. As she shimmied the pants down her legs, she gave an extra wiggle of her shoulders to make her breasts sway.

Cam moaned and stroked the bulge trapped in his black pants. "There's my *konkattie*. Come here."

She loved that he had a pet name for her. She only wished she knew what it meant. The jerk wouldn't tell her, but by the heat in his eyes she figured it must be something good.

Without a moment's hesitation, she floated into his arms where he took her lips in a kiss that made her forget she was standing naked in the dining room. The rough pads of his fingers ran down her spine, sending chills in their wake as he cupped her buttocks and lifted her into the cradle of his hips. His fingertips curled and tickled the seam of her butt cheeks, slipping in the wetness already seeping from her pussy.

He wrenched away and heaved hot, panting breaths into the curve of her neck. "You're so wet for me already. I love that."

Her backside met the icy surface of the tabletop and she

jumped. "Ooo, that's cold."

"I like that too. You nipples poke out so enticingly." He bent her over his arm and took a beaded nipple into the warm depths of his mouth.

Holy cow, he was going to take her on the table.

In any other house, she would have thought that to be a sexy idea, but not this table. This was her grandmother's table. This was the table where family dinners took place, where she decorated her first batch of gingerbread and played pinochle with her grandfather. No way could she allow sex to be had on this piece of family history.

"Cam. Cam, stop." She pulled at the cowl. "Take me to the bedroom."

"But I want you now." He rubbed the ridge of his erection into her wet cleft.

Stars flashed in her eyes. "No. Not here. Anywhere but here."

Beneath the cowl she imagined his brows were drawn tightly together as he stared down at her. For long seconds he watched, and she suspected he was trying to read her emotions. Who knew what satisfied his curiosity, but that wicked glint made the gold in the irises flash. "Anywhere, hmm?"

What did she open herself up for?

A gentle tug on her hand brought her to her feet and across the living room to the big picture window.

"My first choice would be to take you under the trees and make naughty snow angels, but considering the frigid climate, this will have to do instead."

He lifted the blinds and opened the window to the arctic blast outside.

"Motherfuckers," she blurted and wrapped her arms around her body. Mammoth-sized goose bumps erupted over her skin. "I'll freeze to death."

"Hands down. I'll warm you up." He pushed her hands down. The heat from his body took the edge off the chill, barely. "Look how lovely your nipples are. Like ripe, frozen berries."

Between the heat of his mouth and the needlelike pinpricks of cold air, Fiona swayed on her feet. Torn between agony and ecstasy, she closed her eyes to enjoy the hot lap of his tongue.

A palm full of snow hit her left breast and she jumped with a squeal.

"Keep your eyes open." Cam massaged the icy burn away. "Put your hands on the sill. Do not move."

As she braced her hands, she realized she was completely exposed to the neighborhood. Smoke rose from the chimneys in billowy clouds, scenting the air with soot and cut pine. The homes she could see looked dark and empty, but for all she knew, the occupants were glued to their windows with binoculars.

"Cam, this is crazy. What if we're seen?"

He stepped behind her and trapped her in his arms. Both of his hands firmly held hers to the window frame in a silent command to hang on. "What if we are?"

"You'll be spotted."

Cam slid his fingers through her damp folds and her sharp cry echoed over the white snow as if she were wired to a microphone. He held the damp lips apart to stroke his condom-covered cock in her wetness. She felt the rubbery blunt head lodge into her opening then pull away in a teasing stroke.

"If anyone is watching, it is not me they are looking at. They will be hypnotized by the sway of your breasts and the sight of your full lips as you cry out in pleasure. You are most stunning to watch when you're being fucked."

Her fingers curled into the wood as he pressed inside her. Despite her arousal, the cool breeze tickling her skin made her clamp down on his invasion.

"*Jesu*, you feel so good around me," Cam gritted out between tightly clenched teeth. He tilted her hips to his liking and plunged hard and deep.

She bit her lip to hold back the banshee-like wail that burned her vocal cords. The smooth glide of the heavily veined stalk was a pleasure beyond anything she ever read or heard about. Her body was a mass of contradiction, she was hot and cold, melting yet tense, unable to do anything but hang on to the windowsill like a lifeline and ride the tsunami-size wave Cam tossed her on.

"You're holding back." He nipped at her shoulder.

"I'm…" She swallowed hard. "I'm not."

"Scream. I want everyone to hear how good you're getting it right now."

"Cam." His name ripped from her throat.

With his lightning-fast reflexes, he scooped up some snow from the ledge and rubbed it onto the burning bud of her clitoris.

Her scream echoed into the distance, followed by frantic grunts as she tried to catch her breath. "Evil. You're evil."

"By the way your pussy opened up and grew hot, I say you love it."

She did. Heavens above, she did.

Her shoulders lowered as she bent deeper into a forward fold. The sight of her wet, pink flesh sucking on the thick staff impaling her shattered the last of her inhibitions. This was no gentle lovemaking, but a raw fucking, and she wanted more. She loved the look of his strong legs as he braced his weight to take her harder. The way his manly toes bent to grip the floor for greater purchase made the ache in her belly tighten to the point of delicious pain, soothed only by rub of his crown against the hot spot in her pussy.

Cam's need to see her come undone was an aphrodisiac to her senses. With a touch or stuttered breath, he made her feel beautiful, powerful in her femininity. Yet she noticed her passionate warrior was containing his own pleasure, stifling his groans with his mouth pressed tight against her back. If he wanted to hear her scream, he was going to have to reciprocate and allow the broken moans he held back free rein. No way was she going to be the only one incinerated in the inferno of their passion.

With her most sultry pout, she looked back at him over her shoulder and dropped the guard on her emotions. In her mind's eye she imagined stroking her hands over his skin, trailing her lips over the smooth flesh and catching the rivulets of sweat with her tongue. She shimmied her hair so the ends tickled the taunt skin on his lower belly.

His nostrils flared and his fingers tightened on her hips in response.

"Hard, Cam. Harder."

"You're a temptress." He scraped his teeth along her shoulder. "I don't want to hurt you."

"You won't. You'll make it feel so good. You always do." She punctuated her breathy praise with a squeeze of her inner muscles.

A handful of snow against her clit made her squeal with surprise. Chilly water sluiced down her legs, adding another scintillating sensation. Along her back, her spine burned where he lay against her while her breasts and belly stung as flecks of snow melted on her skin.

"That should cool you down." His evil chuckle tickled her cheek. "I want this to last."

"Not fair. Not fair." Damn the man. She needed to come now.

"What's not fair is you melting around me. I bet you're like hot syrup, and those little squeezes are divine."

So was the massage of his fingertips around her clit. He alternated between the pulsing bud and the area stretched around his shuttling cock.

Oh yeah? Two could play this game.

In slow increments she eased her hand into the snow gracing the ledge and turned up the sex-kitten coos and appreciative moans. When her hand tingled with the cold, she reached between her legs and cupped his tight sac. The heated flesh seared her palm as he shouted and shoved hard inside her.

"You little witch. You want to test me? Then reap what you sow."

Cam's hands at her hips were the only thing keeping her upright as his pelvis worked at a frantic speed, lifting her to her toes with each thrust.

Propriety was officially shot to hell as her body rejoiced in the brutal claiming. If the neighbors were to hear her screams or see her receiving the fucking of her life? Who cared? Let the house catch fire or all the pipes burst, she really couldn't give a rat's ass. He might as well have tossed her out the window and into the knee-deep snow bank. The shock to the system would have been just as intense.

Every nerve was alive. Her lungs burned as she dragged in deep mouthfuls of frigid air that exploded out again in a scream. The world dropped away and her vision clouded as she soared. Her only tether to consciousness was Cam's grip around her waist and his own cries of release in her ear.

Nearby the trees shook, falls of snow cascaded off the weighted limbs as his bellows echoed in the distance.

His knees buckled and he dragged her to the floor to sprawl across him. Under her back his muscles jumped and twitched and his chest heaved with his ragged breathing, which delighted her to no end. Cam was the strongest man on the planet, and she wore him out. Little ole Fiona Corrione went toe-to-toe with an out-of-this-world lover and brought him to his knees.

"Is that," she paused to clear her throat, "all you've got, space boy?"

"You want more? Give me five seconds and I'll...still be right here." His arms came around her and she felt the press of his lips against her hair. "You amaze me, woman. With sex like that, I'll be on your doorstep every night when you return from work."

Crap, why did he have to bring up the future now?

Yes, tomorrow would come. And of course she wanted to see him again. She'd be stupid not to crave his affections after experiencing world-altering sex. But what type of relationship were they developing? Friends with benefits? Boyfriend-girlfriend? And what about the Chameleon's responsibilities to the public? How did she fit in with the implied obligations he had with the people?

All those questions, and the ones she was certain she hadn't thought of yet, had to be answered, immediately. Soon. Well, not that day, but definitely in the near future.

"How do you have the energy to think?"

His groaned question startled her from the dark turn of

her thoughts. "Don't eavesdrop on my brain."

"I'm not. I've noticed you grow unearthly quiet when thinking. You should be soft and sated, not tense with uncertainty. Did I do something wrong?"

She tilted her head to place a kiss on his lips. "You're perfect. Well, almost. If only you were able to produce hot water, then you'd be perfect."

The power came back to the house with a swell of energy as the appliances hummed as if they were charging up a hill. Lights she had forgotten she left on blinded her with their glow as she struggled to a stand and reached for a blanket dangling over the back of the couch to cover her nakedness.

Cam stood at a more languid speed, his limbs flowing in a graceful wave that spoke of his confidence and was oh so sexy. "I'd like to take credit for this, but I don't have that power. However, I can draw you a hot bath once the water tank refills."

"Will you join me?" Would he finally remove the cowl and let her run her fingers through his hair?

"While you're relaxing, I'll make us dinner. I want to pamper you this evening."

He wasn't going to take off the hood. Boo. He wasn't rushing off at first light. Yay. A small yay, but she'd take whatever he had to offer.

"I hope this pampering involves a massage."

He pulled her into an embrace. "When I'm done, there won't be an inch of you that is not branded by me."

Her head fell back to allow him unimpeded access to kiss her neck. To their right, the open window framed the mountain and the chain of lights that sparked as power was restored to the rest of the neighborhood. With each yellow flicker her throat tightened and her fingers wanted to curl into his thick biceps and never let go.

The fantasy was coming to an end. For all she knew this was to be their last night together. Oh sure, he said he wanted to see her again, but that was when they were isolated from reality and riding a constant high of orgasms. In the bright light of day all the warm fuzzies currently coursing through his veins could disappear as quickly as the snow melting outside. Look what happened in the movie *Speed*. All that great chemistry between Jack and Annie yet Keanu didn't bother to show up for the sequel. Then again, no one should have shown up for that movie.

If this night was all she had left with him, she wasn't going to waste a second. With a deep breath she went on tiptoe and sealed her lips to his, conveying all the affection she felt for him into her kiss and hoped when morning came, Cam knew her heart belonged to him.

Chapter Seven

"YOU'RE LOOKING QUITE chipper for being elbow-deep in spoiled cream," Aunt Bridget said as she leaned against the open door of the walk-in refrigerator. "Please tell me you waited until daylight before coming in this morning."

"The sun was up long before I was," Fiona replied with a roll of her eyes.

Well, technically the sun had been up when she left the house, but Cam had woken her up extra early with open-mouthed kisses spread over her breast. Never before had she had such difficulty leaving a warm bed. Only their sense of duty, her to her employees and his to the people, nudged them out of her comfy home.

"Then what has you smiling like you discovered a way to eat chocolate cake without consuming the calories? I know it's not joy from cleaning up this mess."

"What's with the questions? We're alive, we survived the storm relatively intact and I have insurance. Isn't that enough?"

Bridget huffed and dragged over a second garbage can. "That's it? I thought it was something juicy, like you met a man."

She lifted a crate of questionable-quality eggs in front of her face to cover her burning cheeks and tossed them in the trash. "In a snowstorm? Really, Auntie, you read too many books."

"I'm optimistic. I bet you stayed indoors the entire week and didn't once go out to play in the snow. At least I got out a little."

"Yeah, I heard," oops, *she* hadn't heard, Cam had, "nothing from you, you know, with the battery dying on my phone and all. What mischief did you get into?"

"Who says it was mischief?"

"Was there whiskey involved?"

Her aunt opened her mouth then snapped it shut. She took a sudden great interest in her fingernails. "Maybe."

"Were the authorities called?"

"No, but Officer Dhavin did stop by. He was checking on everyone in the neighborhood. Once he saw we were fine and dandy, he left us with a jaunty wave."

"Who were you with?"

"Mr. Hendrix, Eliza and the Dursthams. We were having a lovely time until Clive suggested we play strip poker and shucked his clothes before the cards were even shuffled. Nothing kills a party faster than a pair of old-man balls spotlighted with a flashlight."

A carton of milk dropped from Fiona's hand as she burst out laughing. "Eww. I need bleach for my brain. Good Lord, woman."

"I suppose when he was younger, he might have been the stud, but I tell you, he did nothing for me. I think Eliza would have taken him up on his offer, but she's so shy."

"And eighty." Did she really need to point out that fact?

"So what? Old people like sex too. Just not as often. Anyway, I guess it was a good thing you didn't venture outdoors. I ran into Mrs. Miller at the gas station and she thought there might be crazed animals in your neighborhood. She said some wild beasts were fornicating rather loudly last night. Frightened her to tears, she said."

Thank goodness for the cool interior of the refrigerator calming the race of heat scorching her face. So, her screaming orgasms sounded like a wild beast, huh? Lovely.

Fiona shut the refrigerator door and began to drag the garbage cans toward the back door. "I guess I had my earbuds up too loud to hear anything. Sounds like it was quite something. Anyway, it looks like we only lost the milk, cream and eggs. I called around and Hogan's is expecting a dairy shipment at one this afternoon. I'll head out there and be the first in line. If all goes well, we can prep tonight and open first thing tomorrow."

"Good, good. It will be nice to return to normal."

Was a return to normal even possible? If normal meant nights without Cam, then the answer was no, which scared the bejesus out of her. After only knowing him a week, the thought of not seeing him every day left her as cold as an icicle.

What happened to her? She was a modern, independent woman who did not need to be joined at the hip to a man, however being joined to Cam at any point of the body was not an unpleasant thing.

Their relationship, if a week of hot sex counted as a relationship, was new and the excitement that came with the newness was addicting. She only hoped that once daily life commenced, the need to know what he was doing, where he was and counting the minutes until she could see him again would fade away. She just had to be patient and keep her perspective. Like the craving for a chocolate caramel bonbon when you just ate one. Drink a glass of water and wait thirty minutes and the feeling would pass. Work. Lots and lots of work was the cure for puppy love.

Fiona pulled the hood of her coat over her head and leapt across the small river flowing down the alley. Mother Nature's follow-up to the blizzard and wind was a rapid snow melt that turned the streets of Cedar into the canals of Venice. And to think, it was only December. No one would be dry for another four months.

The trip to Hogan's Market was like trying to figure out a life-sized maze. Where she'd normally turn right, she was forced left by a fallen tree. A few more blocks down the road and a flooded storm drain made her change direction again. After twenty minutes and traveling a grand total of one mile, she was almost ready to call it a day and try again in the morning. Almost. The storm had already taken a major hit to her business, she refused to let it take any more.

She took the fourth detour and shouted in victory as an empty stretch of roadway lay before her like a gray piece of taffy. Triumph was short-lived after she rounded the bend and was stopped by an officer blocking the road and motioning for her to stop.

She rolled down her window as he approached. "Hold up for one second, ma'am. We have some debris we need to clear that might come across the road. Won't take but a minute."

"Sure. No problem." She peered over his shoulder and laughed. "That's an entire tree. I think this is going to take longer than a minute."

His jovial chuckle joined hers. "Normally, yes, but the Chameleon is here to assist. You're welcome to turn around, if you wish."

"No." The word came out breathy. "No. I can wait. Maybe even stretch my legs a little."

"Right." He shook his head with a rueful smile that told her he knew exactly what she was thinking. "Just keep out of the way, ma'am."

"Of course."

The wind kicked up as she stepped out of the car and whipped the loose ends of her ponytail into her eyes. She brushed the strands away and her jaw dropped when she spotted Cam a few yards away in the midst of man and chain-saws.

The hard set of his lips pinched tight with strain as he held up the trunk of a hundred-foot Douglas fir. Only the strength of his arms prevented the bulky tree from sliding into the entry of the home that caught the brunt of the collision. An axman slashed the extraneous limbs away with a roaring chainsaw, whittling the mass to a more manageable size.

When the axman gave the all clear, Cam hoisted the trunk over his head and set it down alongside the road like a weight-lifter dropping a loaded barbell. He brushed his palms together and looked up, catching her eye.

Before she thought better of it, she waved her hand with the enthusiasm of a groupie and felt her cold cheeks bunch in a grin.

Cam nodded, his mouth formed a slight grin that was exceedingly polite for a man who had kissed her most intimate areas just that morning. With a small salute he dismissed her with a turn of his back.

The chilly response slapped her in the face like an arctic gale. Her glove felt as if it were weighted with rocks and dropped heavily at her side. She hadn't expected him to bound across the street and greet her with a big smooch, but he could have at least smiled as if he was glad to see her or send her a wink.

She tried not to feel as if he'd punched her in the heart. They'd never discussed what they'd do if they ran into each other in public, so she couldn't blame him for the slight. At least, that's what she tried to rationalize as she squared her shoulders and fought back visions of revenge. She was an adult and possessed the maturity to behave like one.

Then she noticed Cam talking to the sheriff.

The breeze played with the strands of blonde hair that escaped the sheriff's braid, and Cam smiled that smile Fiona thought was just for her as he smoothed the lock back into place. His fingers lingered along her cheek for longer than was professionally acceptable.

The sheriff knocked his hand away, but the corner of her lips twitched and she batted her lashes in a silent message Fiona took to mean, *I like when you touch me, but not now.*

What. The. Hell?

Fiona fell back, dropping into the driver's seat before her knees gave out. No way did she just witness Cam flirting with the sheriff. A very married sheriff whose husband was a fine-looking man in his own right and was probably one of the only people Fiona knew who could challenge Cam in a fight and possibly win. No. The sheriff would not be so foolish as to jeopardize her marriage.

The deep husky tones of Cam's laughter brought her gaze back to the pair, much to her chagrin. The sheriff was gesturing off into the distance, then placed her hand on his arm. Did she just caress his biceps!

Fiona shut her eyes and willed the gathering tears to go away. She was not going to cry over a man. Never.

Yet as the mantra repeated in her mind, she felt her chest constrict and a salty taste gather on the back of her tongue.

A knock at her window brought her out of her mental pep talk with a startled squeal.

The officer held up his hand. "Sorry, ma'am. Didn't mean to frighten you. You can proceed now."

She nodded, too choked up to risk speaking. One wrong move and she felt ready to break into a million pieces.

Argh! This wretched feeling was so stupid. What she and Cam had was a fling. That was all. Deep down she knew that was all they were going to have when she first allowed him through her door. He was the frickin' Chameleon for Pete's sake. And she was…well, her.

But the fantasy. Oh, the fantasy had been so good. Of course she wouldn't want it to end. What sane woman would?

Well, the bubble was officially burst now. The eggs had been cracked and nothing could be done to put Humpty back together again. For a smart woman like her, the best course of action was to move on. Good thing this happened now before she did something über-stupid, like fall in love with him.

She sniffed and looked around the interior of the car. Damn it, where was a crate of tissues when she needed one?

Aunt Bridget would have a coronary if she knew Fiona's thoughts. "Giving up so soon, lass?" she'd say. "Where's your fighting spirit?"

The spirit evaporated the moment he turned his back and cuddled up to the sheriff. And right in her field of vision no less! No way was she going to even contemplate a relationship with a man she couldn't trust.

But she had trusted him, and that's what stung the most. Cam coaxed truths from her she never shared with anyone. Now that connection was gone and she felt the loss as surely as if he cut off her mixing arm.

No, no, no. She swiped at her cheek at the lone tear that escaped and glared at her hangdog reflection in the rearview mirror.

You will not cry over a man. Never.

Never, she repeated during the rest of the day every time her vision blurred and her eyes stung. When the urge to curl into a ball in the middle of the kitchen struck, she plunged her hands in too-hot water, or scrubbed the front counter until the tiles glowed. In the middle of the afternoon, it was an innocent batch of cinnamon rolls that paid the price of her repressed anger.

"What did that dough ever do to you?" Bridget asked as the sound of dough hitting wood echoed around the kitchen.

"It's my favorite part," she muttered as an excuse and imagined the mass of flour and butter was a miniature version of the Chameleon. She lifted the dough over her shoulder and threw it down on the butcher block table with a satisfying grunt.

"Not too hard, dear. We want tender rolls, not rocks."

Rocks would be good. A good pile of rocks the size of softballs that were perfect for throwing.

No. You will not think about that man.

Thwak. Just. *Thwak.* Don't. *Thwak.* Think.

The sky turned dark and Bridget had long gone home while Fiona continued to work, dusting and scrubbing until the shop sparkled brighter than it had since move-in day, probably even more. Every time she thought about calling it a day and heading home, her throat closed up and her stomach rolled. Memories of Cam were branded in every room and every surface of her home. There wasn't a spot that didn't remind her of what she once held in her hands. Perhaps it was delusional to think that Cam could ever be hers. But for a few days he had been.

Whoever said memories kept one's bed warm should be punched in the throat to prevent such silliness to be spouted again.

There was a couch in her office. It wasn't the most comfortable piece of furniture, but would be more than adequate if it meant staying away from home for a while.

"Ugh!" Fiona shouted and slammed the office door shut. The loud crack sounded so good she whipped the door opened and slammed it again.

What happened to not giving that loser a second thought? As if he had a clue as to the turmoil that had rolled through her all day. He was probably out flirting with every woman in town while playing superhero and here she was contemplating sleeping on a lumpy sofa because of a little heartache.

Not acceptable.

"Strong, independent woman. That's what you are," she repeated as she jerked on her coat and tied the sash around her waist with an extra-vicious twist.

She was going to go home, pour herself an extra Irish cof-fee and unwind by watching *The Avengers*. Seeing the Hulk beat the crap out of Loki always made her smile.

As she reached to open the back door, a heavy knock vi-brated the reinforced steel. Since Bridget had a key, Fiona could only guess as to who might be on the other side. A tiny, traitorous kindle of hope flared before she could squelch it to sodden ashes.

"Fiona?" Even through layers of wood and metal, Cam's rich accent had the power to make her quiver. "Fiona, it's me."

The fact he didn't say his name, as if she would automati-cally know who was calling, brought the fight back into her spine.

"Just a minute," she called out, then folded her arms and counted to twenty. "Strong, independent woman."

When her heart rate slowed, she opened the door and leaned a nonchalant arm against the frame. "Cam. What a surprise. What are you doing here?"

The thick brush of his lashes fluttered as his eyes nar-rowed. "I came for you. You weren't at home and I was worried. The question should be what are you still doing here? Did you have storm damage? You could have contacted me and I would have been right over to help."

Her tight smile hid the fangs she wanted to bare in anger. "I don't have your number, remember? Anyway, the only damage we sustained was food related. Everything's hunky-dory."

"Good." He cocked his head. The stiff set in his shoulders warned her that he may be picking up on her anger.

"Well, it was good to see you. Have a good night."

"Wait." He stepped across the threshold before she could close the door in his face. "What is wrong?"

She backed away and stumbled when she hit the edge of the butcher block table. "Nothing. It's been a long day and I have an early start tomorrow."

"Oh." His posture relaxed. "You work so hard, Fiona. Let me take you home and I will help you relax."

She gripped the edge of the counter to keep upright. Damn, the promise in his smile still melted her bones. "That's okay. I can make it home alone."

"But I want to be with you." He closed the gap between them and slid his hands around to cup her backside. "I've thought of nothing but you all day."

"Bullshit." The curse shot from her mouth before she realized she thought it.

Cam froze. "What?"

"Nothing."

"Obviously it is not nothing."

"And obviously you've forgotten about this afternoon."

Trying to disengage from his embrace was like untangling herself from a cat's cradle from hell. She slapped against his chest, but he didn't budge.

He feinted left and right, trying to catch her gaze. "What

about this afternoon?"

Agh. She fisted her hands to keep from tearing out her hair. She refused to become the screechy, jealous girlfriend. The idea made her want to retch. Better to end this entire farce of a relationship now before she became someone she despised.

"Look, Cam. The past few days were great. But it's time to return to reality. You have your life, and I have mine. I understand that, so you don't have to pretend that we're a…we. Us. Whatever. You are free to go on your merry way. Goodbye."

Cam stared at her as if she had hit him over the head with a baseball bat. His chest rose with his indrawn breath and he pinched the bridge of his nose. "I was told Earth women were complicated creatures. I know English is not my native language, but I think you are, what is that phrase, giving me the brush-off? What has happened since I last saw you this morning?"

"I—you—what?" Her ear-piercing shriek drew her up short. "Vine Street? You lifting a huge tree? You looked at me as if you had no clue who I was then went and flirted with the sheriff."

"I did not—" He sucked in a breath and looked off into the distance as his eyes bounced as if he were watching the replay of his day. A second later he breathed out, "Kristos."

"Yes, she's married to Kristos, who I think can totally kick your ass. But that's none of my business, because there is no us, so why should I care if you get beaten to a pulp? Just, oh, never mind."

"Fiona." He was on her in a flash, covering her mouth with his broad hand. "There has been a misunderstanding. My feelings for the sheriff are like what one feels for a favorite cousin. I respect her, and her husband, too greatly to offend them in such a way. And if I did not recognize you earlier, I'm sorry. It's been quite a day today, but please know that I will never ignore you again."

Despite the heavy coat surrounding her, a shiver shot down her back as his hand shifted and the pad of his thumb brushed her lower lip.

"I can't promise that I will be able to greet you as…enthusiastically as I want, but please believe me when I say you mean so much to me. More than you can guess, and more than you may want to believe."

In the shadows of the bakery his words wove a fantasy she never wanted to wake from, but that's all they were. Words.

"Cam. I don't know—"

"That's right, Fiona. No one knows. Please don't be afraid to take a chance on us."

But she was afraid. Terrified.

Was Cam telling the truth? Her heart wanted to believe him, but if he meant what he said, look how one misunderstanding ruined her day.

It hurt her to look into his big, pleading eyes, so much so she had to turn away. But Cam wouldn't let her. His hands cupped her cheeks. That all-seeing gaze of his dared her to look away as he pressed a kiss to her firmly set lips. Again and again he peppered her mouth until she sighed and gave in.

Who was she kidding? A crook of his finger and she'd be there, clothes ripped away, tossed carelessly on the floor, followed by her supple body spread out upon the fabric to wait for his possession.

What a wuss.

"You're thinking too hard." He unbuttoned her coat and shoved it off her shoulders.

"You're trying to seduce me."

"Obviously I'm not doing it correctly."

Heaven help her, he intended to try harder.

His hands sliding down her back and the glide of his tongue along hers communicated his mission to obliterate all her objections. In the quiet of the kitchen, the sound of her breathing was as smooth as one of her stand mixers with a broken whisk, while Cam's was deep and even, heavy like a man enjoying a decadent meal.

He edged the fingers of his right hand under the waistband of her jeans and panties and curled them around her bottom, slipping the tips between the slick folds of her sex. Damn her body for succumbing to his charms so easily.

"Say what you want, Fiona, but I see the truth in you, because it's the same that's in me."

"It's just sex," she choked out the lie.

His answer was to fill her slick channel with his thumb and squeeze the hard bud of her clit. "I won't be satisfied with sex alone. I want all of you, Fiona. But if it's sex you'll respond to, I'll gladly give you what you need."

Not the neck. Not the...ah. Her head fell back as he scraped his teeth along the vein frantically pumping blood to her cloudy brain. He hooked his other arm under her leg, opening her body farther to his hand. Those wicked fingers plunged and pressed, stoking the fire in her loins and causing sweat to trickle down her hairline.

"Think this is good, *konkattie*? Imagine how good we can be together if you'd only let go."

Let go? She was allowing him to finger-fuck her in her place of business. How much more did he want?

Spots danced in her vision and her heart raced as if she were schussing down the longest ski jump in the world. Except there was no soaring off the end and the exhilaration of flying. Nope. Instead there was a wall and she hit it hard, breaking into a million electrically charged pieces that throbbed and ached.

She screamed into his chest. Her fingers flexed into the muscles of his shoulders with only Cam's strength keeping her upright.

"You are magnificent when you come." The husky rasp of his voice sent shivers along her neck. "You are also magnificent when you smile, and when you're reading, or cooking or just being you. Trust me on this."

She had to grasp the edge of the table when he set her back on her feet and bent to scoop her coat off the floor. Confusion furrowed her brow as she watched him. The hard length of his cock was still imprinted on her belly yet he made no move to relieve the ache he must be feeling. He bundled the coat around her, taking care to make sure each button was fastened.

"Cam." She clutched his hand. "You can't make everything better with an orgasm."

His smile was white in the shadows. "How about five?"

"That's an odd number."

"Six?"

She laughed. It was impossible to stay mad at him when he was at his most charming. "I mean that's an arbitrary number. Has five worked for you in the past to get you out of trouble?"

"No, Fiona. I've never had to use sex to get what I want."

"What do you want?"

"You. I'm going to take you home and do more to convince you how much I want you."

Home. He said it as if he thought of her house as his home.

She was beginning to think of it as theirs too.

✦   ✦   ✦

SPARKS FLEW OFF the end of the lit cigarette as it sailed out the window of the car and sputtered a quick death in the soggy grass.

This was good. This was damn good. Trevor punched the number on his cell phone he was told to use only under the direst of circumstances.

"Donovan," came the reply after the tenth ring. At least the call didn't go to voicemail.

"Yo, man, it's Trevor. Get me Smithwick."

"It's Mr. Smithwick to you, Skeeter. And no." The line went dead.

Motherfucker. He hated that nickname. The senior assholes got to name the new recruits and they usually chose a moniker that tended to piss off the recipient.

Trevor hit redial and waited. And waited. And waited. The second the line picked up he shouted, "Fucking prick. I will own you one day."

"Lofty ambition, Skeeter."

"Mr. Smithwick." Holy shit. "I'm sorry, sir. I thought you were someone else."

"You contacted me. Didn't you?"

Trevor shivered in his seat. He didn't know where Mr. Smithwick was from, but the accent was foreign, a mix of Indian and British that sounded cold and menacing, yet undetached at the same time. It was a dangerous accent, like the man could cut you to ribbons and not give a damn. There was no passion, just precision, and it scared the shit out of him.

"Yes, uh, yes sir. I did." He swallowed hard and worked to produce enough saliva in his suddenly parched mouth to continue the conversation.

"Skeeter, my time is money. Do not contact me again."

His gut tightened with the knowledge that if Mr.

Smithwick cut the line, his life would be cut next just as quickly.

Spill it quick, bud, or dig your own grave.

"The Chameleon has a girlfriend."

Silence.

Trevor held his breath, willing that the soft whoosh in his ear was Mr. Smithwick breathing on the other end of the line.

Sweat gathered on his brow and trickled into his eye, but he didn't make a motion to take a swipe at the drop.

"Continue," came the reply in a tone that was just as cold as before, yet held a light note of intrigue.

"Well." Trevor shifted to a more comfortable posture in his seat and ran the sleeve of his shirt over his forehead. "I figured the Chameleon would be out today helping with storm stuff, so I tracked him down and followed him around and saw him going into one of the shops in town. It's a bakery owned by a chick named Fiona. When they left, I followed them right to her house where they went inside. Together. He's still in there now."

"And you are certain they are a couple?"

"Yes sir. Saw them through the window of the shop myself. He had his hand down her pants and had that bitch howling good." A tingle shot through his own cock as the memory of Fiona's legs thrown over that man's huge forearm flashed through his mind. Damn, he didn't know the frumpy baker could be so hot.

"Keep me posted. The second he leaves her residence, call

me."

"Yeah. Yeah. Will do."

"You've done well. Mr. Skeeter."

Trevor slapped the steering wheel in triumph. *Mr.* Skeeter. He was a mister now. Ha. Before long Donovan would be kissing his ass and taking orders from him.

He reached for the handle of his seat and reclined just far enough to be able to see the lit window on the side of the house. His zipper rasped loudly in the dark as he took his cock from his jeans and gave the shaft a firm squeeze. Hey, if the Chameleon was getting some ass, he could indulge as well. Wouldn't that be something? The Chameleon's ho on her knees, sucking his prick while he made the fucker watch.

Now that fantasy was almost as good as taking Donovan's place at Mr. Smithwick's side.

✦   ✦   ✦

DHAVIN LET HIMSELF into his cousin's house and closed the door behind him with a loud slam. "Kristos. Quit fornicating and get out here. I must speak with you immediately."

"Uh, good morning?" Brett greeted him in the hallway in her pajamas and sex-tousled hair. "One morning, Dhavin. One morning a week I'm allowed to sleep in. Do you have any respect for your superior?"

"I have a great deal of respect for you, but we are not on duty. Therefore you are not my commanding officer at this time. Sorry, cousin."

She emitted a sour grumble and shot him a glare over her shoulder as she disappeared into the kitchen. "You say that now, but wait until you're assigned to Breathalyzer enforcement duty for a month."

Oooh. Dhavin cringed. Normally verifying photos from the home monitoring systems wasn't so bad a task, however Mr. Johnson thought it was funny to take his test completely nude. A seventy-year-old's half-erect penis was not a pleasant sight.

No bother. Fiona was worth Brett's retaliation. "I wouldn't have come, except this is an urgent matter."

"This better be good, cousin." Kristos greeted him with a solid smack to the back of the head. "Your key is for emergency use only."

Dhavin watched with envy as Kristos kissed his wife on the cheek and set about making a pot of coffee. They moved in harmony, each anticipating the other's needs. After all these months, it still took a moment for him to adjust to the sight of Kristos with hair the same blond shade as his mate. During the mating ritual, more than the couples' emotions melded together. Their hair and eye color changed, with one gaining the other's coloring, to identify the mated pair. The last time he had seen Kristos on Skandavia, his hair had been as blue-black as his brother's.

He tried to imagine what outcome a mating with Fiona would produce. Their coloring was very similar already. Would she even notice the bond if he spoke the words without her knowing?

"Dhavin." Kristos' shout drew him out of his musings like being dropped in a pool of ice water. "I'm five seconds away from allowing my wife to whip you with her pistol. Tell me what is so important."

"Sorry. I have a lot on my mind." He took the offered cup of coffee and waited for Brett to take her seat before he announced, "I met a woman."

Kristos raised a light brow. "That's it? I thought you meet women all the time."

"You make it sound like I go prowling for female companionship when you know that is far from the truth. I meant I met *the* woman. My future mate."

Brett chuckled into her mug. "Would this be the woman you mentioned the other day?"

"The same."

"I take it you were able to change her opinion of you."

"Yes. Well, no. Um...not exactly."

She heaved a sigh as her head tipped back. "What is it with the men in your family? Why can't you woo a woman like normal men? At least have the decency to tell her you are going to tie your emotions together for eternity before you actually do so. Give the girl a fighting chance."

"May I have some credit? I'm not like my *borehund* cousins. My woman will be fully aware when I speak the Sacred Vows."

"Who's the girl?" Kristos buttered his toast without acknowledging the slight against his courtship practices.

"Fiona Corrione."

Brett gave an uncharacteristic squeal of delight. "From The Sugared Thistle? I love that shop. And Fiona is so nice, but quite the ball-breaker from what I've heard. So what is it you're not telling us?"

He sucked in a breath and held it while he thought of the best way to approach his dilemma. His mouth dropped open and twisted in several attempts and with each try, he realized the size of the hole his deception had dug.

"You see, she refused to accept a date with me, so when I discovered she had an interest in the Chameleon, I pursued her from behind the mask."

Two sets of pale-green eyes stared at him with a mixture of confusion and disbelief.

"Pursued her? How?" Kristos asked. "What, you walked into her shop dressed in the royal uniform and said, 'Hello. I'm the Chameleon. Would you care to join me for a meal?'"

"Not exactly. We had a few encounters, one aborted date, but grew closer during the storm."

"Aha, that's where you went every night, instead of going back to Harlan's," Kristos crowed.

"He was safely ensconced in the city with Lucian and Amaryllis, and even if he wasn't, I would have carried him myself to you here in order to spend the night in Fiona's arms."

"Wait, wait, wait." Brett waved her hands. "You had sex with her?"

"Yes."

"With the mask on?"

"Obviously."

She sighed and pressed the pads of her fingers against her closed eyes. "Let me see if I've got this straight. Fiona would not agree to a date with you as Dhavin, yet she has spent time with you as the Chameleon, intimate time, and doesn't know who you really are?"

Thank the Gods, she understood. "Yes!"

"How is that possible? She doesn't have a clue that you and the Chameleon are the same man?"

"No. And I have not sensed any realization on her part."

"And she's never seen you as the Chameleon without the mask? Never asked about your origins?"

"She said that my secrets are mine to entrust with her when I feel she's earned them. I find her understanding to be among her most appealing traits."

"What secrets about the Chameleon has she earned?"

There was an undercurrent to Kristos' question that raised the hair on his arms. For all the trouble the family had gone to in protecting their origins, his cousin's query was valid.

"Most of them. To a point."

"You hedge questions like a junkie shielding their supplier. Straight answers, please."

"I've told her about Skandavia, but that I'm the only one of us here on Earth."

"What have you told her about our," Kristos pointed at

both of them, "arrival to this planet?"

"An abbreviated version of your story."

Kristos swiped a hand over his face. "Fantastic."

"I trust her and I will tell her the entire truth. Eventually."

"When?"

"Once I have her trust in me, which is why I am here. Yesterday she saw you as the Chameleon and you didn't acknowledge her."

"Maybe because I wasn't aware we were dating."

"What was more damaging was she saw you two flirting. She believed the sheriff was having an affair."

Brett backhanded Kristos in the arm. "I told you to cool the touchy-feely when we're in public."

"Then stop looking so sexy in your uniform."

She dropped her head in her hands. "Fuck. Do you think anyone else saw? How many other people think I'm a cheap slut?"

"Calm down, *alskata*." Kristos rubbed his hand down her spine. "I don't believe anyone thinks that. Fiona was probably hyperaware of the Chameleon's actions and misinterpreted what she saw."

"Or so we hope," she muttered.

"No. Now she understands that the only affection is the kind one has for family." Dhavin hoped his smile was reassuring, but Brett didn't look convinced. "In the meantime, Kristos, if you see Fiona again, please remember she is the love of your life and treat her accordingly."

"Excellent. Does that mean I can suck her tongue down my throat?"

"No!" came the heated response from him and Brett.

"It was only a suggestion."

Brett stood with a disgusted sigh. "I don't see how the *Llanos* line has continued this long if the men were like you. Have you given any thought to how Fiona's going to react once you tell her the truth? Which you are going to do any day now, right?"

"She'll understand."

"You hope. I'd wish you luck, Dhavin, but I think you are going to need a miracle." She kissed the top of his head on her way out of the room. "I'm off to the shower. If I lose my access to her salted caramels because of my association to you, I will retaliate."

Brett's certainty that he would fail to win Fiona's heart made Dhavin truly question his actions for the first time. Of course he didn't want to lie to her, but she made pursuing her so bloody difficult, what other options had there been?

He dropped his head in his hands and peeked at his cousin between his fingers. "Have I truly fucked up, Kristos?"

Kristos drew in a breath. "Define fucked up."

The hot breath of his groan dampened his palms.

"Don't fret yet. Tell me true, cousin. Are you Fiona's?"

"Yes," he replied without hesitation.

"Not so fast. Think on it. To tell her the truth involves putting more than yourself in a potentially dangerous situation.

The secret of our people does not rest solely on you."

As much as he hated to admit it, Kristos was right. Dhavin closed his eyes and looked deep into his mind. He pushed aside the memories of Fiona's lips brushing his skin and the velvet clasp of her body holding him tight, for it was more than sex he wanted to share with her. Instead he focused on the soft smile she wore when listening to his stories, the way her eyes narrowed when she concentrated on a task. He thought about how she loved her family and the way she treated the customers in her store as if everyone were special.

"Yes. I am hers. When I am with her I feel...home, if you can call it that. I don't think that is an emotion here on Earth, but with her, I feel whole."

"I understand exactly what you mean." Kristos' gaze flitted to the door his wife had departed through. "Now, is she yours?"

Any warmth he felt at the memories of Fiona dissipated as if Kristos had snuffed out the flame. "I'm not as certain as I once was. But I have to try. If I don't, I will regret it for the rest of my life, and believe me, I have done many things I should have regretted and don't, but this, I know will haunt me forever if I don't at least try."

Kristos smiled and slapped him on the back. "Then I am happy for you and will do anything I can to ensure your success. You have sacrificed everything for this family. It is the least I can do."

"Thank you."

"In fact, I'll start now by checking on how much ice we have, because I see a ball-kicking in your future."

Dhavin flashed him a tight smile and an obscene gesture even as his gut tightened with the knowledge that his cousin may be correct.

Chapter Eight

I am obligated to work late this evening and cannot make
our date. Hate to disappoint and promise to make it up to
you. Tomorrow? All night? I need to feel you close.

C

FIONA FROWNED AS she read the text for a third time and
tried not to give in to disappointment. Only Cam could
provide his brand of help, and it wasn't his fault he was needed
elsewhere. Plus there was the promise of being in his arms for
the entire night once he was through. How could that not
make up for the slight delay?

"What's up?" Mags asked. "You look like someone told
you Santa Claus doesn't exist."

"My plans fell through for the evening, but we're resched-
uling. It will be fine," she said and slid the phone into her back
pocket.

She never carried her cell phone on her during the day, but
since Cam gave her his number and started texting her, the
device never left her side. It was pretty juvenile, waiting with
bated breath for any type of communication, but the few short
texts she received meant so much, knowing he was thinking of

her as much as she was him. Who knew he was so good at sexting, or that she loved the naughty talk as well? Earlier he had sent a photo of a full moon and a promise of how he'd make love to her under the pale-blue light. His words had made her wet in an instant and she had to blame the red in her cheeks to the heat of the oven.

"So, are you going to tell me who this mystery man is?"

"No."

"Ah, come on, Fiona." Mags followed her around the shop, sounding more interested in digging up gossip than helping with dusting the displays. "I want details. You've been getting some, girl, and I'm dying to know who has put that glow in that smile you've been blinding me with for days."

Was her happiness that obvious? "It's new and I don't want to spoil anything."

"Well whoever it is, he must be good. Does he have a brother?"

"Drop it, Mags. Can you start closing down the kitchen?"

"Fine. I'll let it go, but you won't hold out forever. A girl has got to dish, and sooner or later you'll need an outlet. I can bide my time." She pointed at her eyes with two fingers and back at Fiona in an *I'll be watching you* gesture.

"Don't hold your breath," Fiona called out after her.

The bell over the door rang and she turned to greet the new guest. Chills ran down her back as she watched the lone man turn a slow circle inside the door while running his fingers through his long, greasy hair as he surveyed the room.

A shudder shook her before she put a clamp on the knee-jerk reaction.

It wasn't polite to make a snap judgment based on a first impression, but men who wore oversized, long-sleeved flannel shirts and torn jeans were not her usual clientele. Especially those whose eyes scanned the room as if he were casing the joint. Cam may be the one with empathetic powers, but right then, her inner alarm was screaming.

She wiped her hands on her apron and focused on slowing her heartbeat. Maybe he was just a kid looking for a birthday present for his mother and he'd be out as quickly as it took to pick up a box of chocolates.

Right, 'cause he looked like the kind of person who remembered his mother's birthday.

"Hello," she greeted with a plastic smile. "Can I help you?"

He turned in her direction and the slow grin that stretched his lips made her swallow hard and her stomach clench with apprehension.

"Yeah," he said with a little laugh and sauntered toward her in a poor imitation of Jim Morrison's swagger. His gaze fell to her breasts and he licked his lips as if he found what he wanted to sample. "Yeah. You can…help me. I'm looking for something sweet to eat. Something really tasty I can fill my hands with and rub my face in."

Now she could judge him. Verdict—Mega-creep.

He approached the counter and rested his hands on the surface, leaning over in an obvious attempt to look down her shirt. Obstinacy kept her hands at her sides. She was not going to give the little turd the satisfaction of knowing he bothered her, but she did take half a step back.

"What you see in the case or on the shelves is what we have. Nothing else."

He laughed again and took a quick glance at the sweets. "What's your favorite, baby?"

Oh no he didn't.

She controlled her repulsed shudder. "The pannatone."

Actually, it wasn't, but at twenty dollars a loaf it was the most expensive item in the store.

"I'll take one."

"Fantastic."

She made short work of wrapping up the bread for transport. "That will be twenty-two eighty."

He gasped. "For an oversized roll?"

"It's really good bread."

"Baby." He handed her a couple of bills. "For that much money, it better make me come."

Eww. She clutched his change tighter to keep from dropping it on the ground. No way was she going to bend over in front of him. As she placed the money in his upturned palm, he grabbed on to her wrist.

"Wait a sec, doll face. Let me get a look at your hands. With all of this dough to work with, I bet you really know how to use them."

"Let me go," she said in a tone one reserved for a disobeying dog while inside her blood curdled at his clammy touch.

Politeness only extended so far. Who did this punk think he was? Thank God Mags was only a scream away.

"I may feel better about my purchase if I got a little extra sugar to go with it." He tugged on her arm and leaned over the counter.

Panic burned in her throat like acid as his grip tightened. "You haven't touched it yet. I'll take it back and gladly return your money."

His gaze traveled back to her breasts. "I don't want money from you."

Customer service be damned. She opened her mouth to scream and the front door sounded a welcoming chime.

Officer Dhavin stomped into the store. He braced his hands on his hips, pulling back the tails of his coat to expose the gun in the holster within easy grasp.

"Good afternoon, ma'am," he said while leveling a glacier glare at the boy. "Trevor. I'm surprised to see you here. Doesn't seem like your type of a hangout."

Trevor let her go with a slow glide of his palm along her hand. "What man doesn't like a treat now and then? Thanks, baby." He winked at her. "I'll be seeing you."

Fiona reached for a bar towel and wiped off the sticky residue of his touch as she watched him amble to the door.

"Take it easy, pops." He brushed past an immovable Dhavin and whistled on his way out.

"Friend of yours?" she asked with the first easy breath

she'd had in minutes.

"Frequent visitor at the jail. Mostly for breaking and entering. He's not very good at it. Did he hurt you?"

"No, he just gave me a serious case of the heebie-jeebies."

"What are those? Is that a disease? Does he need to be quarantined?"

Man, Dhavin really wasn't up on his slang, but his genuine alarm made her smile. "No. It means he made me feel dirty and uncomfortable. Other than that, I'm unharmed."

"Are you certain? I can have him detained for the night, just because."

"That's okay. I appreciate the suggestion."

Mags burst through the kitchen door in a cloud of perfume. "Officer Dhavin, I thought I heard your voice."

Seriously? Now is when Mags decides to make a grand entrance? Where the hell had she been when a creep was molesting her boss?

Dhavin bent forward in a slight bow. "Good afternoon, Margaret."

Then silence.

And more silence as the giant wall clock ticked away in loud beats.

Fiona felt her eyes widen as she stared at the handsome officer. Where was his usual flirty banter? Was he sick?

Mags blinked a few times with confusion furrowing her brow then regained her smile. "I was wondering when we would see you today. You're usually here earlier."

"Yes. We're a man down tonight and I was asked to work overnight. My shift starts soon, but I wanted to stop in and talk to Fiona."

"Oh." Her brow puckered more and she shifted her weight from one foot to the other. "Well, um, I bought a new perfume the other day. It's called Wild Nights. What do you think?" She pushed out her chest and tilted her head back in invitation.

Dhavin's feet stayed planted. "I noticed your fragrance when you entered. It's very lovely."

Fiona watched the awkward exchange with the same fascination she had for bad reality television and wished she had a bucket of popcorn. She had expected him to laugh and bend close to the young girl, brushing the tip of his nose along her skin before delivering a cheesy, but charming, line about how he found her delectable. This polite and aloof version of Officer Kilsgaard was definitely a departure from his flirtatious self, and apparently not to Mags' liking.

With each attempt Mags made to engage the officer in conversation, Dhavin responded with clipped answers that made her eyes flash and lips purse in annoyance. Fiona had to place a hand over her mouth to hide her shocked amusement before she burst out laughing. Oh this was horrible. Hysterical, but horrible.

After Mags threw a Hail-Mary Pass move that included showing Dhavin her latest yoga trick to which he responded with a polite nod, she issued an exasperated grunt and tossed her ponytail over her shoulder. "Well." She flashed them both a tight smile. "I've finished in the back. Do you still need me, Fiona? I have a date tonight and I plan on blowing his mind." The narrowed glare she shot at Dhavin was probably meant to make him jealous but ended up appearing more childish than sultry. "I could use the extra time to get ready."

"You can go. Thanks for your hard work today."

She nodded then turned with a huff and her nose lifted in the air.

"Damn," Dhavin said. "I didn't mean to hurt her feelings."

She didn't want to pry, really, but curiosity loosened her tongue. "What was with the cold shoulder?"

His eyes widened with horror. "You thought I was cold?"

"Well, for you anyway. You were very polite and usually you're more flirty."

"I wasn't trying to be mean." He ran his hand over his face with a deep sigh. "I've come to realize that my friendliness and desire to make others happy might be perceived as more than I intend. I'm trying to be more mindful of my words and actions."

"Wow. That's...wow." Whoever heard of such a phenomenon? A man who made a conscious effort to change his behavior? She had absolutely no comeback for that. "What made you come to that conclusion?"

"A good friend pointed out what I was unable to see. I appreciated their honesty." His slight smile held secrets she wanted to be brave enough to ask about. "Anyway, Cam asked me to check on you and see if you received his message."

"Yes. I did."

"He feels horrible for canceling."

"I understand. I'm sure late-night missions occur frequently in his line of work."

Dhavin nodded, but his eyes didn't look convinced of her answer. "Are you certain you're not upset?"

"Of course." She bit her lip before admitting a truth she'd been struggling with all day. She needed to talk to someone and at the moment, Officer Dhavin was the only person she could confide in. "Actually, I'm sort of glad he was called away. I've been thinking we need some time apart."

"Why? What has happened?"

She shrugged and shot a pointed look in the direction of the kitchen.

"Mags is gone. I heard the door slam a minute ago."

"Oh. Wow, you've got good hearing."

"Please, Fiona, tell me what's wrong."

She shrugged again and set her focus on wiping down the espresso machine. It was easier to spill her guts without looking him in the eye. "Nothing and everything. I keep thinking that what we have can't continue. I mean, what are we doing? Are we a couple, are we having an affair? And what about next week or next month? I understand his need for secrecy, I really do, but how long can that last? I feel like I'm in limbo right now and it's not a fun place to be. I think some distance may be what we need to put things into perspective."

"I don't understand." He came closer and stopped on the

other side of the counter. "Don't you enjoy being with him?"

Enjoy? Such a pedestrian word compared to how she felt. "Yes."

"Do you care for him?" The light in his eyes turned hopeful. "Maybe, even love him?"

So much so she was ready to cry, and therein lay her dilemma. How could she be in love with someone she didn't really know? "I care for him a lot."

"Then what is the issue? I know he cares for you too. Is it you want more? What? I'm sure if you tell him, you will find he wants the same thing you do."

"Right." Her harsh bark of laughter sounded bitter in her own ears. "For how long? He's...he's, well, you know, not normal. God, the things he's must have seen and done. I make cookies for a living. Sure, he enjoys my company now, but he'll get bored. And it's not like we can mix things up and go out together because of the mask, and—" Her breath caught as the deepest hurt broke free. "He doesn't trust me with his identity. What if he never does?"

"He will." The fervor in Dhavin's voice surprised her. "Just...give him time. Did you ever think that he may be struggling with the same things you are? That maybe he is unsure about asking you for more because he doesn't want to rush things with you?"

That gave her pause. "I guess I'm still in disbelief that he finds me interesting at all."

"Fiona, at times I want to shake you. Do you really have no

idea how spectacular you are?"

How could she not when a handsome man looked at her as if he wanted to lay her on the counter and devour her whole.

"When the other party in question is a superhero, it's hard to compete."

"Believe me, Cam is lucky to have you."

His compliments brought heat to her cheeks and she had to turn away from the admiration in his gaze. "The whole situation is surreal. Masked crusader. Dowdy human. For Pete's sake, we were even trapped in a snowstorm. It's like a bad Hollywood movie script. How can I trust that anything either of us feels is real when it's all been one big..." She couldn't finish the thought. It was too depressing.

"Cliché."

"What?" Something in his tone brought her head around.

"What is the word? Cliché?" He looked into the distance then nodded. "Yes. That is it."

Maybe it was the accent, but with that one word, she swore Cam was standing before her. She squinted to blur her vision and focused on the flecks in his brown eyes that sparkled like gold flakes and the line of his lips, noticing for the first time the slight dimple on the right side.

Just like Cam.

There had only been a handful of occasions when Fiona felt frozen in time. When her heart and lungs stopped functioning and nothing, not even the air seemed to move. The last occasion was when she first met the Chameleon and now that freaky sense of déjà vu cemented her into place.

All the times she'd been in Officer Kilsgaard's presence, she'd been too shy to meet his gaze. Now, as she looked upon him fully for the first time, the oddest thought struck her so hard, if it would have been a two-by-four, it'd have broken bone.

"Fiona?" He braced his hands on the counter as if ready to vault over the top to her side. "Are you all right?"

Her breath came back in a burning rush. "What? I— what?"

"What's wrong?"

"I—" No. The idea was ludicrous. A crazed laugh bubbled up her throat. To speak it out loud would prove her insane. "I, uh, for a moment I had this panicked thought that I had forgotten to turn off the stove this morning, but I had cereal, so of course I didn't. Ever had one of those weird moments? Really, I'm fine."

His frown deepened and the muscle in his jaw ticked. "Are you sure? I sense all is not well."

She fought to control the widening of her eyes. Cam could sense her emotions too. If he and Dhavin were the same, then he knew she was lying.

Brushing aside his concern with a wave of her towel, she backed away. "I mean it. I'm okay. But I should probably check to make sure Mags turned the ovens off like she said. Better to be safe than sorry." She turned to run into the kitchen, then whipped back around to point her finger and demand, "Don't go anywhere."

He placed his hands on his hips as if to argue but nodded in agreement.

Once in the cocoon of the kitchen, she leaned against the wall and braced her hands on her knees as she fought for breath.

What the hell was she thinking? It wasn't possible. There was no way Cam and Officer Kilsgaard could be one and the same. What did they have in common? Besides a tall, muscular build, a sinfully sexy accent, and they both pulled the late shift at work on the same night?

Oh. My. God.

Don't freak out, don't freak out.

Deep breaths. Deep breaths. She had to keep her emotions under control and think this through. Her head swam with the extra oxygen but her heart began to slow its thunderous beat.

Be rational and think. The Chameleon appeared in Cedar way before Dhavin arrived in town. And she'd seen them standing side by side with her own eyes. It simply was not possible, unless Cam had a twin. Or Dhavin.

Or…Dhavin had a cousin. An equally tall and well-built cousin.

Fiona drew up short as the events of the day before came back. She remembered the confused wave Cam gave her before he went and made goo-goo eyes at the sheriff. Sheriff Briggs had been the first person to have her life saved by the Chameleon. Now she was married to Dhavin's cousin. Maybe there had been more than one person who had come to Earth and now they shared the title to throw off suspicion as to who was behind the mask.

Holy crap. It was sounding logical.

"Fiona." She jumped when she heard Dhavin's shout. "Are you all right?"

"Yeah. Mags left the mop bucket out and I almost tripped over it. I'll be just a minute."

She rubbed at her lips as her brain raced to make sense of her crazy thoughts. It wasn't as if she could march out into the shop and ask him if he was the Chameleon. Would he even tell her the truth if she did?

Her hands moved from her face to behind her neck then down her sides until she passed over the swell of her buttocks. The bulge of her cell against her palms gave her an idea. She withdrew the phone and pressed the reply button to Cam's last text.

"Hit the freaking H," she ordered her trembling fingers through clenched teeth.

Hey. Just got message. Sorry for delay. No worries about 2nite. Looking forward to tomorrow. Be safe.

She pressed "send" then crept to the doorway to peek out to the shop. Dhavin was watching the entrance to the kitchen with his arms crossed and a serious frown line bisecting his forehead. Suddenly his eyes widened and he jerked. After a quick scan of the room, he retrieved his phone from his belt.

Fiona bit back a gasp and watched with her heart pounding behind her ribs as he read the display then released an adorable smile. After another glance toward the kitchen doorway, he typed a response. His thumbs flew across the keys with an inhuman speed then he tucked the phone back into his pocket. A second later, her phone beeped and she jumped a foot in the air, the phone slipping from her grip. The black rectangle bounced from one hand to the other like a hot potato, almost hitting the floor before she wrestled it back against her chest.

With one eye closed in trepidation, she looked at the display.

One new message.

She drew a deep breath in through her nose and pressed the button. Her stomach clenched tighter when she saw it was from Cam.

You are the best. Will most definitely see you tomorrow. Until then I will be thinking of your kisses and the tight clench of your body around mine. Be safe, *konkattie*. If you need me for any reason, any at all, contact me or Officer Kilsgaard. Do not hesitate. Be safe as well.

The promise in his words made her nipples bead as the implication hit her like a cast iron skillet dropped on her foot.

She had sex with Dhavin Kilsgaard!

All this time she'd been ridden hard by the town beefcake. How could she not have known?

Even if she was horribly wrong about his identity, the image was now there. When she'd think of Cam without the mask, it'd be Dhavin's face in her mind's eye, gazing down at her with fire in his eyes, of *his* weight pressing her into the mattress as he thrust his cock deep inside her.

Agh! She pressed the heels of her hands into her eyes to scrub away the picture. Spots floated in her vision from the pressure and the lack of oxygen to her brain as she began to hyperventilate.

A gentle hand fell upon her shoulder, but she leapt forward with a shriek as if she'd been electrocuted.

"It's me, Fiona." Dhavin held up his hands. "Just me."

Damn it. Who the hell replaced the normally steadfast woman with this weakling who started like she was trapped in a haunted house while high on mushrooms?

She pinched her lips together and mentally lassoed her frayed emotions. *Keep it together, girl.* "Sorry. You startled me."

"And you are frightening me. Please, tell me what is the matter." He reached for her hand. The calluses on his palm sent shivers up her arms. These were the same hands that had caressed her entire body and teased her to orgasm more times than she could count.

She wrenched her gaze away from his big hand and was immediately ensnared by the worry on his handsome face. The tender look made her heart melt even as she wanted to scream "liar" right into his face. How dare he act as if he cared about her when there had been nothing but lies between them?

Space. She needed space before she blew up like Mount St. Helens and made herself appear even more stupid then she felt.

"I am feeling uncertain at the moment," she answered in a slow, modulated voice. She spoke enough of the truth to hopefully deflect his ability to sense her falsehood. "I've experienced a lot this week, and this evening has been interesting, to say the least."

"You look pale. Damn, if only I didn't have to work, I'd take you home immediately. Can I call your aunt for you? I don't think you should be on your own."

"No." She pulled away from his touch. *You don't have the right to comfort me.* "I'll be fine. Nothing that some space and time alone won't put to rights." And a big bottle of wine. The smile bunching her cheeks felt as plastic as a pair of wax lips. "Don't worry about me."

Dhavin rubbed at his jaw. "Why don't I believe you?"

"What?" She placed her hand over her heart and batted her lashes. "Why would *I* lie to you?" She pushed against his shoulder, turning him to face the front door and guided him out of the kitchen. "Now go. The people of Cedar are waiting for your protection. And if I unexplainably find myself in trouble, I'll call Cam."

Under her hands she felt him still, the muscles of his back tensing. She held her breath and waited. Would he come clean about his identity now?

Her fingers flexed to dig into his back when he stepped

away and glanced at her over his shoulder. "If you need anything, call. No matter the hour. Promise me."

Her vocal cords stopped working, refusing to speak any more lies, so she nodded.

His lips parted, but he stopped short and pinched them together. She watched him walk out the door and followed behind him, waiting at the window until she saw him round the corner before her knees gave out and she slid to the tile floor, creating the saddest window display in history.

The cool glass was refreshing on her hot cheek and distracted her from the nausea rising up her throat.

There was no question in her mind. The knowledge went beyond her gut. It was as definitive as DNA.

Dhavin tricked her. He knew how she felt about him, yet he used her attraction for the Chameleon to trick her, seduce her and make her fall in love with him.

Honey, you could have said no at any time.

"Shut up," she groaned.

Who cared if her libido was right? She was the wounded party. Of course she always had the power to say no. There had been a million chances to demand more from him and make him take off the mask, or just walk away. But the fantasy had been too good to let go. For one moment she wanted to touch the sun, even with the risk of incineration. Now the sunburn went straight to the bone.

Oh, how he must have laughed with his cousins about the frumpy Earth-girl who dropped her panties with a flash of his smile. How many other women had he duped so easily, or was she the only one gullible enough to fall for the Captain America persona?

As the flames of embarrassment licked up her neck, she couldn't decide which was worse, knowing the truth about her hero or facing the moment when she'd have to confront him with his dishonesty. Continuing the charade was not an option. Look how well she controlled her emotions not five minutes earlier.

God, what was she going to do when she saw him again?

"Wait a minute." She stared off into the distance as inspiration struck.

The question wasn't what she was going to do, but what *wasn't* she going to do.

From the pit of despair rose an idea so crazy, it lifted the hair on her arms. Hysterical laughter bounced around the empty shop like marbles being poured into a glass jar. Defeat turned into indignation that straightened her spine and brought her to her feet.

Her Scottish heritage taught her how to hold a grudge forever. The Italian side, an appreciation for revenge.

Dhavin thought he had her wet and panting in the palm of his hand, did he? The entire week he encouraged her to embrace her sexy, feminine side. Now was the perfect opportunity to show him how well she learned her lesson. He wanted a sex kitten? She was going to make his wet dream come true, and when she was done, he'd be left on the curb with the rest of the trash.

Chapter Nine

FIONA'S HANDS SHOOK as she picked up a log to throw on the fire then dropped it back onto the pile. Up, down, up, down. Indecision had her playing yo-yo with the piece of wood. The interior of the little hunting cabin she borrowed was freezing, but a sheen of sweat gathered along her brow as her insides vibrated as if a swarm of bees took up residence and bustled with activity—their stingers poked her confidence and upset her stomach.

Screw it. She dropped the log and went into the bathroom to look over her appearance for the twentieth time in ten minutes.

To pull off this grand scheme she was going to have to get her shit together and calm the fuck down. Dhavin was scheduled to arrive any minute and everything had to be in place.

"Cam. Call him Cam," she muttered at her reflection as she twisted the band holding her hair at the nape of her neck into place.

After what she spent on supplies, the last thing she wanted to do was blow the entire plan to hell because she called him by the wrong name. Who knew restraints could be so pricey?

If all went as planned, every penny would be well spent.

Battery-operated lanterns bathed the wood-paneled walls in a soft white-yellow light. She had wanted the romantic glow of lit candles but decided against it for safety reasons. The Andersons were kind enough to lend her the cabin on short notice and she didn't want to repay them by having the place burn down if the situation got out of control.

Not that she was planning on starting an altercation with Cam, but the reason she chose a neutral location was in the event she needed a quick getaway. Instinct warned her that once she confronted Cam about the truth, only dynamite would blast him out of her house. The man was freakishly persuasive when it came to getting what he wanted. This way she could lock the door before he ever breached inside.

The gentle knock on the door might as well have been the pounding of a battering ram by the way she nearly jumped out of her skin.

"Easy. Easy." She took another glance in the mirror and drew a calming breath. Determination smoothed her brow as she prepared for an Oscar-worthy performance.

She crossed the two steps from the miniscule bathroom to the front door and pressed her ear to the wood. "Who is it?"

"Cam. And thank you for asking first."

She opened the door and took in the sight of the Chameleon standing in the doorway in all his masked glory. As always, the only parts of his face that were visible were his eyes and his nose and mouth, but the sexy tilt of his lips and the wicked promise in the brown gaze unmistakably belonged to Dhavin.

Yep, she was the biggest idiot on the planet.

How did she not recognize him at first sight? Had she been brain dead all this time? What about the rest of the town? No way could she be the only one who saw what was beyond the rippling pecs, although if she was, she'd feel slightly better about being duped. Very slightly.

With the truth now literally staring her in the face, any remorse she harbored over what she was about to do disappeared as quickly as a grain of sugar in a rainstorm.

"Come in." She stepped back to allow him inside. "I thought a change of scenery might be nice. It's not much, but I think it's cozy."

Cam barely glanced at the extra-large futon made up in satin sheets or the butcher block table decorated with fine china. His hot gaze drifted over her from her neat ponytail down to her freshly polished toes. Under the black lace that covered her breasts, her nipples hardened, tenting the white cotton shirt she secured under her bust with one button.

"Wow. What gods did I please to be gifted with you?" He was on her in a blink, his big hands cupping her buttocks under the hem of her shirt and lifting her against his erection.

For half a second she basked in the heat of his kiss, yielding to the strength in his arms before her ego kicked her in the ass.

She pulled back with a gasp. "So, I guess you like my outfit."

"I never thought a man's shirt could look so sinful, or you

so beautiful. There's a purpose I sense in you tonight. A confidence I find intoxicating." He leaned down for another kiss.

"Not so fast. I have lots planned for us tonight. Come." She untangled from his embrace and gestured for him to take a seat at the table. "I made you a treat."

"You are my treat." He wrapped his arm around her waist and pulled her across his lap.

She slapped at his hands but straddled his legs, making sure to press the hot pad of her pussy against his cock. Good Lord, she shivered, he was hard already. "You're such a horndog. I worked really hard to make this especially for you. It's a super-secret family recipe that has been passed down for generations. I've been told that if a man eats one slice, he can stay hard all night long."

His laughter rumbled in his chest. "And this is a family recipe?"

"They had to do something to stay warm during the cold Highland nights."

"*Konkattie*, I can stay hard just by looking at you."

Flattery would have gotten him everywhere the day before, but now she knew the score and refused to melt under his sizzling charm. She had a plan and she'd stick to it if it killed her.

"Ta-da." She lifted the top of the cake carrier with a flourish, revealing a creamy, dreamy chocolate tart. "Here, let me feed you."

She scooped up a healthy spoonful and held it to his lips with a sweet smile that widened when he eagerly accepted the treat.

He chewed once, twice, then his eyes widened with panic. She swore he was going to spit it out, but he swallowed with a loud gulp. His lips trembled into a weak grin.

"That, uh, that is a taste I've never experienced." He spotted the glass of merlot on the table and snatched it up, downing the entire contents. "What is in that, exactly?"

"I told you, it's a secret. Here, have some more. Delicious, huh?" She shoved another spoonful in his mouth and bit her lip to hold back her laughter as he gagged. "Oh, all right, I guess I can trust you with a little part of the recipe." She leaned close to whisper, "The secret ingredient is black licorice."

"Ah." He coughed into his fist. "That explains that intriguing flavor."

Eat it up, lover-mine. She swirled the spoon into the thick concoction and prepared for another assault.

He caught her wrist and deftly removed the weapon from her grip before she was able to force another large spoonful into his mouth. "You know what this recipe can use, is more salt."

He smeared the dollop of cream across the upper curve of her breast then bent to lick the area clean. Man, that was a smooth move, she'd give him that.

Revenge and desire engaged in a knock-down-drag-out fight in her heart with each flick of his talented tongue. After all was said and done, she still wanted, no craved, his touch and affection. That hadn't changed since she learned the truth.

Syrup filled her veins and pooled in her loins in a delicious burn. Temptation demanded she grind against his erection, take her orgasm and leave him hanging on the edge, but the risk of detouring from the plan was too great to feed the need for physical satisfaction.

Deep down in her soul, she wanted to believe there had been something real about their relationship, at least something other than the way he made her body electric, but the romantic in her was going to have to go without. This night was about revenge, not what might have been. To see her plan to the end, she was going to have to shut down the part of her that held out hope, and she'd better do it quickly before everything got shot to hell.

"Cam." She dug her fingers into the cowl and grasped at the hair beneath to pull his head up. "Cam, wait. I—I have something I need to talk to you about."

"I'm listening." The tip of his tongue danced along her collarbone. He slipped her shirt off her shoulders, allowing his fingers access to the clasp of her bra.

"No. Really. I've been thinking a lot lately and I have to tell you something before we continue." Her breath stuttered as he cupped her breasts over the lace and tugged firmly on her nipples. No, no, no. He was not going to distract her. "Cam, I've been lying to you."

He stilled with his lips pressed against her shoulder, and

she froze along with him. Tension snapped between them like an invisible net for a long minute before he raised his head to look at her with a wary eye. "What do you mean?"

This is it. Don't break character. "I've lead you to believe something about me that wasn't true, because I was afraid of what you'd say. But I like you, Cam. Really, really like you, and I don't want there to be any more lies between us."

His lips tightened and he nodded for her to continue.

A giggle tickled her lips with what she was about to say, but she pressed on. "I know the sex between us has been on the stale side and ho-hum."

"Excuse me?"

If only she had a camera ready to capture the look on his face. Priceless. "Oh, I don't entirely blame you, Cam, I mean, you've been trying so hard to make it spicy and exciting, and believe me, I've loved every minute of it. But the truth is, I want more."

"More?" he asked, clearly baffled. What must he be thinking?

"I've led you to believe that I'm shy when it comes to sex. But, actually, I've been hurt in the past by men who have felt threatened by my intense sex drive. Those experiences have made me gun-shy on showing my true self. I want more with you, but I'm afraid of what you might think when you find out…" She closed her eyes and with a dramatic sigh exclaimed, "When you find out I'm a slut."

He tilted his head. "I do not know this word."

Dear God, please let her say this with a straight face. "A slut is a person who loves sex. A lot. My pussy is constantly wet and aching, desperate to be filled, and I think dirty, nasty thoughts all the time." *Don't laugh, don't laugh.* She pressed her breasts into his chest and leaned over to whisper into the fabric that covered his ear. "The things I dream about doing to your cock, hmm, scandalous. I want to rub it and suck it deep into my mouth. I want you to slam it into me hard and rough. And your cum. God, I want to bathe in your cum."

Never before had she spoken such profanity, but maybe she should have done it more if she received this type of reaction. His hips rolled, grinding his cock that had swelled so hard and hot, there may as well have been nothing between them from the way she felt every ridge pressed against the pad of her pussy. His skin was on fire, burning her palms, and his breath billowed over her chest in hot puffs. Who knew a few choice words could skyrocket him to the edge so quickly?

Buoyed by his reaction, she played up her trampy side, enjoying the illicitness of her words as much as he. "I want to share my fantasies with you. If my needs are something you can't handle, tell me now and it ends here."

"No! Tell me. I want to hear them. I want you, Fiona. Every wicked bit of you."

"Well…" She slowly swiped her tongue along her bottom lip. Her cunt wept more cream as his eyes traced the movement. This was going to be so good. "I want to tie you up. I want you at my complete mercy and to do dirty things to you.

But I know that will never happen." She finished with a pout.

"Why not?" he panted. Dismay colored his whine and threatened to make her break character.

"You have super strength. Even if you let me, you can break out of your bonds whenever you wish. That defeats the purpose of having you at my mercy."

"I won't. I promise, I won't," he said with the eagerness of a child tempted with a new toy. "Tie me up."

She fluttered her lashes with mock astonishment. "What? Surely you don't mean that. What type of man wants to be dominated by me?"

"This one."

"But you'll break away the moment you don't like what I'm doing."

"I won't. I promise," he begged so sweetly. "Please, Fiona. I'm all yours."

"Really?"

"By the Gods, woman. Yes!"

Suck-ah.

Never before had it been so difficult to hold back a smile and victorious fist pump as he folded like a cheap napkin at an all-you-can-eat barbeque.

"I'm trusting you to keep your word, but you've made me so happy. Come stand by the bed." She pulled him to his feet and positioned him by the futon, praying the simple wood structure maintained its integrity, for it was about to receive the ultimate workout. "From now on you have to do everything I say. Everything. Understand?"

He nodded and licked his lips as if he were too excited to speak.

"Good. I'm going to undress you. Don't lift a finger."

She took her sweet time removing his clothes. The tunic was surprisingly heavy when she made him bend down enough for her to lift it over his head. Simply wearing the garment must be an exercise of its own. With each article removed, she brushed her fingertips over his skin, smiling as the muscles twitched with her touch. Standing behind him, she slipped her fingers up his spine and under the cowl. He tensed under her hand and she waited for him to tell her to stop. When he didn't say anything, she smoothed her hands along his shoulders and down his arms. Goading him into revealing his identity now was not part of the plan.

"Lie down," she instructed and reached for the strap trailing from under the mattress.

"Why do I have a feeling the straps are a new addition?" he teased, but complied with her wishes.

"I wasn't sure if you'd agree or not. If anything, I was hoping you might want to tie me up, but this is much better."

The leather straps were notched like a belt, which she was banking on to restrain him better than those with a Velcro closure. After each wrist was secured, she stepped back to admire the buffet of manliness spread out before her.

In the lantern light his bronze skin looked burnished, like every inch had been lovingly polished to perfection. He was lean in the waist and thick everywhere else a man should be. His muscles flexed, but not with the intent to impress, but with excitement and the restraint to allow her to do her worst.

Holy cow. This was the best idea ever in the history of ideas. Tremors ran down her limbs and her brain worked at a feverish pace, trying to decide where to begin in his sensual torture. Between her thighs, her panties, soaked beyond reason, chaffed her skin.

She began by laying her palm flat on his chest. On either side of her hand his two hearts pounded a thunderous beat and his legs jerked impatiently.

"Fiona, you're killing me."

"That's Mistress Fiona." She raked her nails to his navel and dipped her thumb in the well. "Don't make me punish you by leaving you with nothing but air to blanket you."

His belly shook with his laughter. "My apologies, Mistress Fiona."

"I think I need to occupy your mouth." She retrieved the pie and set the pan on the floor by the bed. Swiping two fingers into the cream, she painted his lips until they were covered.

She bent down and began lapping at the sticky substance as if she were starring in a raunchy comedy movie, slobbering with more enthusiasm than finesse. As she feasted, she ground her lace-covered crotch against his inflamed erection, working her hips to imprint the texture of the fabric onto his flesh. She thought he would be put off or shocked by her behavior, but

Dhavin surprised her by engaging his tongue with hers in play and biting at her lips.

A case of the giggles threatened to crack her tough-girl façade, so she pulled away and slipped her bra from her shoulders. The hard points of her nipples tingled as she dipped them in cream and placed one into his waiting mouth.

Her eyes crossed as he suckled hard, drawing the entire areola between his teeth, which made her smirk. Now the taste of black licorice didn't bother him so much, huh? If he loved it on her breasts, how about on her pussy? Didn't he say the recipe needed more salt?

The useless scrap of her panties hit the floor and the cool pie filling she spread on the smooth lips of her drenched sex made goose bumps ripple down her arms. Her legs shook as she climbed back onto the bed and straddled his face, facing his feet and the bobbing erection that pulsed with each heartbeat. Before she had a chance to settle into positions, Dhavin lifted his head and dove into her open cunt. The sloppy sounds of his mouth against her wet hole had her fingers curling, her nails digging into his abdomen for purchase.

A steady stream of pre-cum leaked from the flared head of his cock and his hips bucked, fucking the air. Fiona gripped the base and squeezed hard, drawing a vibrating groan from his chest that tickled her clit.

"You don't get to come yet. This is for me. Lick me clean. Yeah, that's it. Fuck me with your tongue," she shouted, getting into the spirit of her character.

Hell, who was she kidding? Even though she was mortified at the smut spilling from her lips, acting like a flaming slut was liberating on so many levels. The filthier she spoke, the harder and deeper Dhavin ate her pussy. He was a wild beast devouring his prey and reveling in the feast, his fervor spurring her own.

"I'm gonna come on your face. Make me. Make me come, bitch." She slapped his flank then froze with shock.

Oops. Perhaps she was taking things a wee bit too far. Her thighs tensed, ready to jump off the bed before he broke free of his bindings, for there was no way he would accept such treatment.

Dhavin proved her wrong as he groaned into her cunt and pressed the hard nub of her clit against the roof of his mouth, shoving her into the whirlpool of an orgasm that rippled up from her core, bathing her in a wave of heat that felt as if she were being dipped in hot wax. Her screams of release echoed in the tiny cabin until they tapered off into warbling moans.

Her joints melted and she collapsed onto his heaving chest. The drowsiness fogging her mind was so delectable, she wanted to drown in its sweetness. What was her name? Where was she? Who cared, she felt absolutely fantastic.

Consciousness pushed through the thick layer of satisfaction, forcing her to open her eyes. The giant red cock weeping cum an inch from her nose brought her back to wakefulness. Right. Revenge. She wasn't done with him yet.

Well, maybe a small reprieve was in order. Her arms were

beyond noodle-like, lifting her just high enough to drag her breasts across his lap as she slipped off the bed and landed on the floor like a sack of flour.

"Whoa." She climbed to her knees. "Give me a minute. Don't go anywhere."

Her lungs slowly returned to normal as she collected the supplies from underneath the bed. She sucked in a few more breaths to relax her trembling muscles. Phase two of her plan required steady hands or else the night would go to hell.

"Lift your hips," she instructed and laid a towel onto the mattress under his butt.

Once he lowered back down, she lifted a pair of eight-inch-long metal scissors, opening and closing them with a wicked snip-snip sound.

For the first time that evening his eyes narrowed with genuine concern. He tugged at the restraints on his wrists and his cock softened. He didn't lose his erection by any stretch of the imagination, but his cock lay against his belly instead of saluting up to the sky.

"Fiona. I'm sorry, Mistress Fiona. What are you doing?"

She ran the flat length of the cold steel along his shaft. "Don't question me. This is my fantasy."

Snip-snip.

Dhavin watched her with wide eyes. His breath puffed out in sharp bursts, which led her to believe he'd never had an intimate haircut before. She took extra care in clipping the hair at his groin down to the skin. Not even she was so cruel as to dive right in with the razor without properly preparing the area first.

After he was shorn to her liking, she brushed up the mess and wrapped a warm, damp towel around his cock. With the scissors safely tucked out of sight, he melted into the mattress, his legs falling open and a deep sigh rumbled from his chest as his eyes closed in relaxation.

Poor schmuck, did he think she was finished? Hell, she was just getting started.

His eyes flew open when she chuckled with wicked intent and cracked open the packaging on a brand-new four-blade razor. She whipped away the warm towel and blew a cool breath across the toasty pink skin. One hand worked the shaft while the other massaged his sac in firm strokes that had him groaning and jerking at his restraints.

Just as the pre-cum began to pool at the tip, she pulled away and reached for the can on the floor. She flashed him a smile as she worked some shaving cream into a lather in her hands and slathered it over his dick, stroking her hands up and down to add more steel to his hard-on.

"Don't move," she cautioned as she held up the razor. "Remember, this is my first time."

At the touch of the blade against his pelvis he froze and they both held their breath as she made the first stroke. The second and third followed then she cleaned the razor in a bowl of hot water and continued with her work. As the minutes passed, Dhavin's muscles loosened as he relaxed, and his low moans filled the tiny cabin. In her grip, his cock firmed, pulsing in her palm as she shifted the length this way and that, moving the skin of his testicles to ease her progress as she worked all the way down to the area around his dark hole.

She took her time, giving the task her utmost focus. The objective was sensual torture, not a punishment that ended up with a trip to the emergency room. Every so often she glanced up at his face and smiled at the way his eyes flashed with heat and passion, his gaze riveted on the movements of her hand. Once he was free of hair and cream, she paid special attention on cleaning the area well, and moved the tools to the table.

Time for part three of the plan.

She turned back to her slave and had to grab on to the edge of the table as her knees buckled. She felt her eyes boggle as she got her first good look at the anaconda writhing against his belly and his large testicles that tightened the longer she stared.

Dhavin moaned. "*Jesu*, Fiona. I can come from the feel of your gaze alone."

She couldn't catch her breath. Dear Lord. That monster fit inside her? Without the covering of hair, his cock looked as if it were two inches longer and wider than she could encircle with one hand. She was hypnotized and terrified by what she created, but helpless to resist the allure to touch and taste the rosy-pink flesh.

Kneeling between his thighs, she pressed her tongue against the smooth skin under his ball sac and near his anus. His hips shot up, nearly dislodging her, but she hung on, working her tongue in slow circles around the orbs and sucking each into her mouth. Her hands worked the shaft, stroking up and down and over the weeping knob of the crown, using her thumbs to open the little slit farther apart to dip her tongue in every few licks.

Dhavin moved like a live wire, jerking and shaking in his leather restraints. Words fell from his lips she didn't understand. The language was foreign but for a few distinct curse words she recognized. Soon it became a game for her to see what strokes of her tongue brought forth the most heated curses. Holding the crown against the back of her throat with a wiggle of her tongue along the underside of the shaft caused him to moan low in English while quick flicks of the tip under the sensitive glans made him shout in the lyrical language she guessed was Skandavian.

"Fiona," he groaned and gasped when she squeezed the base hard in warning. "I mean, Mistress. I'm near to coming. I'm—I'm—ah."

She jumped off the bed so fast, his hips kept bucking, unaware she no longer had him in her grasp. It wasn't time for his orgasm.

Her hands trembled as she opened the foil packet and withdrew the condom. Man, she hoped it was large enough. Part of her was tempted to double bag his cock, but even she wasn't that vindictive.

By the time she rolled the rubber over his flesh, Dhavin was thrashing, his eyes closed tight as he begged for relief. And all because of her.

The power she had over him at that moment was an aphrodisiac so intense, she wished it came with a warning label. Caution—will cause shakes, dizziness, shortness of breath, severe leaking from the pussy and an insatiable need to be filled.

Her sheath clenched and ached, expressing its displeasure of being denied for so long. His size no longer frightened her, in fact she hungered to slide down his pole and ride him hard.

They both watched as the crown parted the lips of her sex and lodged at her entrance. Working her hips back and forth, she took him in deeper and deeper, the stretch burning with delicious heat until her bare pussy kissed the smooth skin of his sac. She braced her hands on his heaving chest and slid up and down, driving all thoughts of revenge from her mind as the pleasure consumed her. On each downstroke her breasts bounced and the flesh of her buttocks rippled, but she didn't care. She was a woman fucking her man, hugging him in the most intimate of embraces. She, plain ole Fiona Corrione, had a strong warrior with superpowers from another planet between her thighs, under her body, and had him mindless with passion.

Sweat pooled in his sternum and wet the fabric of the cowl touching his face. His thighs were slick and her hands slipped off his chest as she rode him faster.

His dark gaze met hers and her pussy fluttered with impending orgasm. "Forgive me," he said.

Before she could think to question him, he wrenched forward, snapping the leather straps and scooping his hands under her buttocks.

He bounced her on his lap, driving his cock deep and grinding his pelvis into her swollen clit. She felt as if she were strapped to a rocket sled, hurtling down the track at Mach 8. Her heart pounded, pressed to his sweat-slick chest as he rocked her up and down. Her mouth worked open and shut, desperately struggling for air.

Then she hit the wall at the end of the track and shattered. Every molecule in her body burst like a supernova and she felt as if she were tossed from her consciousness, floating above them to view their two bodies as they slammed together in carnal bliss. Her sheath clamped down and gushed so much moisture, it shocked her even though she was out of her mind.

"Gods, I can feel you come on my balls." Dhavin groaned, his teeth clenched tight in concentration. "Hate this condom."

Unbelievably, his cock hardened, growing thicker and stealing the last of her breath.

"Never again, Fiona. Next time I'm taking you bare." His thrusts became frantic. "I'm going to fill you with my seed. Forever, Fiona. You. And. Me."

The blood rushed in her ears, drowning out his roar as he came, filling the condom with his cum as his cock twitched and stroked the nerve endings in her sheath to another orgasm.

Tears spilled from her eyes and the anger she kept leashed

burst from its confines. She lacked the breath and energy to shout, so she bit his shoulder, drawing blood, for he had spoken out loud the very dream she had begun to hold in her heart.

Forever.

It was a beautiful thought. Forever holding, kissing, loving each other. Joining their lives and making babies. Motherhood had never been one of her aspirations, but lately the thought was in her peripheral vision. She had wanted to carry Cam's child and give him the family he had given up when he came to this new world.

But those dreams were about Cam, not Dhavin. Who was this man who shuddered in her arms and held her to him as if to absorb her into his skin? Was he a man she could love?

Did she even want to find out?

Chapter Ten

WHEN DHAVIN HAD crashed through Earth's atmosphere his body had gone through transformations so intense he had been left pulverized and had to relearn how to move his body to accommodate his new powers. That experience had been like a shot of B-12 compared to a night spent under Mistress Fiona and far less transformative.

For the first time in his life, he was whole. The part of himself he had believed he'd left behind on Skandavia was found. Yes, his cousins meant everything to him. It was why he risked his life to save them. They were his family, but they weren't *his* family. With Fiona at his side, those dreams were soon to become a reality. He found his home.

By the Gods, his woman was filled with surprises. Incredulously his cock stirred as if he hadn't been drained to his marrow in one of the most sexually intense experiences of his life, which was no small feat considering his best friend owned a sex club.

With one hand, he cupped his swelling shaft while the other blindly reached across the mattress in anticipation of what she had planned for breakfast.

Cold sheets met his palm. The chill worked down his spine like a warning beacon.

He sat up with a jerk and spotted Fiona standing near the foot of the bed.

Mistress Fiona was long gone, and the way she was dressed, wearing jeans, boots, scarf and a winter coat buttoned up to her chin, Dhavin wondered if he had dreamt the entire evening. Only the sticky residue on his flesh and the smooth skin around his groin confirmed the events of the night before.

Her cold, vacant stare drew his balls up into his body. Whatever thoughts were going through her mind were not good. Under the mantle of determination that kept her shoulders straight, she carried a sadness so profound it made his hearts ache. It was as if she had lost her best friend.

"Fiona. What is it?"

Her mouth opened then shut. Several times she appeared ready to speak but stopped short. Each attempt tightened the anxiety in his gut until he couldn't breathe.

"You know." She paused and closed her eyes. The derisive laughter that puffed from her lips didn't lessen his tension. "I've been thinking of what I would say to you at this moment for a while now, but I don't think there's anything that will make me feel better, so I'll just leave it at goodbye. Goodbye, Dhavin. It's been…real."

Dhavin?

What was the phrase? Ah, yes. The shit was hitting the fan.

"Fiona." He leapt from the bed, blocking her path to the

door as she stepped toward the exit. "Wait. I don't understand."

"Are you kidding me?" she screeched. "Look me in the eye and swear you're not Dhavin Kilsgaard."

"I—" Cold air burned his heaving lungs. "I. Can't."

He reached up and pulled off the mask covering his head. Even though not a stitch of clothing covered his body, removing the hood left him feeling exposed in ways he had never experienced.

Fiona's eyes widened and her breath hitched. The determination he had sensed in her earlier increased tenfold. She swirled a finger, indicating his face. "I rest my case."

He sidestepped to block her again. "I was going to tell you the truth."

"When? Tomorrow? Next month? On your deathbed? On my deathbed? After you knocked me up?"

"No." Although that would have been nice. His thoughts must have shown on his face for she gasped in outrage and stomped her little foot.

"Look, if you don't mind, I'm trying to keep this civil, so goodbye."

He allowed her to march out the door so he could pull some pants on. His cock was not behaving in an appropriate manner and needed to be pinned down for his brain to begin to function fast enough to match her wit. She had only taken three steps toward her car before he swept her up in his arms and deposited her back in the cabin. The door swung closed with a solid thud behind him.

Jesu, how did this morning became such a clusterfuck?

"You must give me the chance to explain. The Chameleon is not my secret to bear alone. If you know who I am, then you know who my family is. I couldn't risk their identities by telling you the truth so early."

"You think I haven't thought of that?" She pushed against his chest for him to release her, but he kept her in the circle of his arms. "Look, I'm not upset because Cam kept his identity from me. I'm angry because you," she pushed her finger into his sternum, "Dhavin, tricked me. I told you I wasn't interested in going out with you and you used your powers to sense my emotions and manipulated me to get your way."

"That's because you wouldn't give me a chance to court you properly. You believed I was arrogant and deceitful."

She snatched the cowl from his hand and waved it like a flag. "Thank you for proving my point."

"The only thing I've lied about to you is my role as the Chameleon. Everything else has been true."

"All of it?" She crossed her arms in challenge. "Every word?"

"Yes."

"Are you really from a planet called Skandavia?"

"Yes."

"Were you really a royal guard?"

"Yes."

"Were you banished for not protecting the queen?"

"Actually, that was Kristos."

"I'm outta here."

"Wait." He gripped her by the shoulders, dropping his hands when she slapped at his wrists. "Kristos was the one who was banished, as was Lucian. I came to Earth to warn them about a plot to end their lives. If I told you about my journey, you would have guessed the truth about Kristos and Lucian."

"Don't remind me of them. I'm sure you've all had a good laugh over the stupid Earth-girl."

"Is that what you think?" He didn't need to ask. The sour taste of her embarrassment coated his tongue and curdled his stomach. "Never, Fiona. Believe me, I have not found any part of this deception humorous. The reason I've been hesitant to tell you the truth is because I feared this very moment. I did not want to see you look at me like I physically struck you. The fact I've caused the woman I love pain wounds me deep."

"You don't love me. Those are pretty words Dhavin would say to charm a woman."

"No. I mean what I say." He took her hand and placed it on the center of his chest. "My feelings have always been true. I love you, Fiona. And I know you love me. We can make this work."

Her fingers flexed on his skin, pressing gently into the muscle before pulling away. She looked up at him with eyes that shimmered as if she were looking at him from the bottom of a wishing well. "You're wrong. I loved Cam, and he doesn't exist. I don't even know who Dhavin is. And I don't think I want to know."

"Fiona."

She dodged his outstretched hand. "Leave me alone. Please. If you come near me, I'll tell the sheriff one of her deputies is harassing me. Don't push me on this."

Dhavin let her go although everything in his being screamed at him to drag her back again and use the broken straps to tie her to the bed until she saw reason, but he needed to rebuild her trust and riding roughshod over her wishes now was not going to help his cause.

Anger and embarrassment dictated her actions now. In time she'd come around. He wouldn't accept less.

As the heavy cloud of her disappointment hung in the air like a musty perfume, Dhavin shivered with uncertainty. Perhaps a talk with Brett on how human men grovel at their woman's feet was needed.

✦   ✦   ✦

DHAVIN COULDN'T DECIDE what was worse. The ache in his chest from where Fiona ripped out his soul, or the burning in his groin where a five o'clock shadow was appearing on his balls. There was little doubt in his mind that this torture was exactly what Fiona had intended when she planned her grand seduction. Crafty minx.

The icepack on his crotch and the beer coursing through his blood soothed a little of the fire in his loins. The blaring television was mindless distraction, passing away the minutes until he could walk without a limp. Yet despite the discomfort, a sense of hope buoyed his spirits. In order for Fiona to be this vindictive, she had to have been hurt deeply, which meant she had to care just as deeply.

Plus, there were her parting words that replayed in his mind every time he shut his eyes. She didn't think she wanted to get to know Dhavin. Not want. Think. If optimism was all he had to cling to, then he'd hold on until every sinew in his arms disintegrated and dropped him into the well of oblivion.

With time her wound would close and he could begin his courtship again. He'd give her just as long as it took for the burning to subside before he launched his pursuit. By midnight, she'd be in his arms.

"Dhavin," Kristos bellowed from outside. The heavy pounding of his boots on the front steps rocked the house. "Where are you, you lazy arse?"

Dhavin reached for a throw pillow to settle across his lap, but he was too slow for Kristos who used his key and speed to open the front door.

If it hadn't been directed at him, Dhavin would have thought the stunned look on Kristos' face was hysterical.

"By the Gods," he sputtered and pointed toward the ice pack. "Your woman nailed you in the nuts."

"No. She didn't." He sank deeper into the couch and closed his eyes. That amused look on his cousin's face was as painful to bear as his laughter fizzing across his sensitive skin. "Leave, please."

"Are you kidding? And miss out on the details? When Brett told me you called in ill, I had to come over. What happened?"

Dhavin released a heavy sigh. "Fiona figured out I'm the Chameleon."

"How?"

"She's a smart woman. I'm actually proud she knows her lover so well she could no longer be fooled."

"Well bully for you." Kristos crossed his arms. "Can she be trusted with our secret?"

"For certain. She's more angry that I used the mask to seduce her than over the knowledge of my identity. She won't tell anyone."

"Ah, so she did nail you in the nuts."

"Will you stop saying that and leave me be? Honestly, I think I would have preferred she physically struck me than the actuality."

The grin that lit his cousin's face tightened Dhavin's grip on the plastic bag. "What *did* she do to you?"

He closed his eyes and focused on his breathing. If he ignored Kristos, then Kristos didn't exist. Of course, with his eyes closed he missed the moment his cousin leapt into action, snatching the icepack and holding it high in the air from across the other side of the room before the warm air touched his jeans.

"Give it back." Dhavin hobbled across the room and

jumped for the bag.

Suddenly they were children again, with Kristos holding one of his treasured warrior figures over his head and daring Dhavin to reclaim it. But they weren't boys anymore, and he was no longer the runt of the family. He had skills he was not above using against relations.

He pinned Kristos' arm to the wall and landed a jab to his stomach followed by a head butt to the chin. Kristos' grip loosened enough for Dhavin to gain control of the bag, which he quickly tucked down into his jeans. He dared his cousin to try to steal it now.

A warrior howl sounded a nanosecond before Kristos tackled him to the floor, wedging his knee into Dhavin's back and the other across his left shoulder. Cubes of ice dug into his pelvis as he bucked and writhed, trying to dislodge the two-hundred-and-thirty-pound man off his back. The smooth grain of the hardwood floor held no traction under his palm that slickened with sweat from the exertion.

Kristos wrestled a thick arm under his windpipe and flexed. "What did she do to you?"

Spots floated in his vision. "Get off me, you smelly disease-infested *bourhund*."

"Oh-ho. If you can insult me, then you can talk. Confess, lad. I have nowhere to be. Do you still require ice? Here, let me assist you." He pressed with his knees, digging the sharp cubes into his groin.

"You fucking prick," he eked out of his crushed windpipe.

"That's a good American insult. What else have you got?"

His lungs burned and the ability to compose a really good comeback was nonexistent. Tears leaked from his eyes to pool on the floor beneath his head. Lucian had once pinned Kristos in this same fashion when he tried to steal Lucian's favorite cruiser. Even when Kristos passed out, Lucian held his position until he regained consciousness and questioned him again. Kristos learned from the master and Dhavin hated to admit the truth that Kristos would not release him until he yielded.

He pressed his face into the floor with defeat and mumbled, "She shvnebe."

Kristos leaned closer. "I apologize. Can you please repeat that?"

He sighed. "She shaved me."

"What does that mean?"

He needed an explanation! "She scalped me, all right? Now the hair is growing back and it burns. Happy now?"

The sudden rush of air to his lungs burned just as badly as his throat as Kristos jumped to a stand. "Was this before or after she told you she knew you were the Chameleon?"

"Before."

"Are you serious?"

Dhavin glared at him over his shoulder and rubbed at his throat.

The laughter welling through Kristos started slowly, then built like a fuse on a bottle rocket before shooting into the air with a loud crack. His knees buckled and he braced his hands on the floor as he continued to howl.

Let him laugh, Dhavin thought as he lay on the floor, huffing for breath like a fish out of water. There was a story about Kristos that involved Brett, a pair of handcuffs and a chain that sapped their strength. Odds were his cousin would find himself in a similar situation again. Oh, how Dhavin wanted to be the one to bail him out then.

He turned his head as he heard Kristos speak.

"Lucian." He had his phone to his ear. "You won't believe what I just heard."

The peal of laughter that vibrated out of the phone after Kristos retold recent events had Dhavin gritting his teeth. Now his humiliation was complete. Who knew Lucian had the ability to laugh so hard?

"He's on his way here." Kristos pocketed the phone. "He said he wants to be here in person."

Dhavin raised his fist and made a gesture that told Kristos whose ass he could go screw.

"You must really be in love with this girl if you allowed her to come at your manhood with a blade." He held out his hand and helped Dhavin rise to his feet.

"I do." He flopped back onto the couch and closed his eyes. "I hurt her feelings. Understandably she's upset, but it will pass. This is but a small hiccup in our relationship. I am not giving up on her yet."

"Good. I hope you know that we, and I do mean all of us,

are rooting for you. If you need us, call."

"I will. Thank you."

"Got any more of those beers in the kitchen?"

"Nope. Not a one."

"Right. I'll help myself." He turned to leave the room and paused with a knock on the wall. When Dhavin met his gaze he asked, "Given the opportunity, would you let her do it again?"

There was no question what "it" was. The memory of Fiona, naked and flushed, kneeling between his legs with her pink lips stretched over his throbbing cock replaced the fire in his groin with a heat of a different sort.

Kristos chuckled. "I'll take that smile to mean you would."

In a heartbeat.

✦   ✦   ✦

FIVE O'CLOCK WAS the latest he allowed himself to stay away from Fiona. He didn't want to think of the upcoming encounter as a confrontation, but he was ready to fight for their future. If a knock-down drag-out match was what it took, then the gloves were off.

He stopped by the shop first to see if she was steeping herself in work to avoid him. The store was dark and closed up tight, so he made his way to her home. The little house was just as black inside as the store had been. There was the possibility she decided to hide out at her aunt's house, but something about the stillness in the air made his arms tingle and his brain jolt with a rush of adrenaline. As he rushed up the driveway he saw the front door stood slightly ajar. The lock was broken and a muddy footprint was stamped on the blonde wood.

Silence filled the house, the sinister weight clung to him like cobwebs as he crept from room to room. His didn't sense anyone in the house, but that didn't mean a malicious visitor wasn't waiting to attack.

The sight in the living room made his muscles tense and his hands clench, ready to smash skulls. An armchair lay on its side and all the knickknacks from the mantel were scattered across the floor, mingling with shards of a broken lamp and pieces of firewood. A search of the rest of the house found nothing amiss, which made his hearts race faster as he realized this wasn't a burglary.

He pulled out his cell phone to call Brett and froze when he saw a white envelope on the dining table, propped up against a crystal vase holding a blood-red rose. Scrawled across the parchment in an elegant hand was one word. *Chameleon.*

His chest felt as if it were filling with concrete, weighing him down in a quick-drying dread, and his hand trembled as he reached for the envelope and withdrew the thick notecard from inside.

Dear Chameleon,

Darling Fiona requests you join her at the old Millstone building in the city. This is an intimate affair, so only your presence is required. She is waiting patiently for your arrival, but I must say I am enjoying her company tremendously. In fact, the longer you dally, the better acquainted she and I become. I heard her sweets are quite delicious and I'm feeling the need for a nibble.

I look forward to our meeting,

S

Dhavin crushed the paper in his grip. This was his worst nightmare. Hell, it was everyone who wore the mantle of the Chameleon's worst nightmare. As a police officer it was expected you hunt and detain criminals as part of the job. Threats were often made toward those on the force and their families, but there was a solidarity in the department. But as the Chameleon, he was on his own. Any fallout from his actions landed squarely on his shoulders. And this time it grabbed Fiona in its spiteful grip, using her to punish him for his contributions to the community.

Gods, he had been so stupid. Why did he think his alter ego had no effect on his personal life? He should have taken more care to protect his privacy and his woman. Actually, he should have done a lot of things, but now his priority was getting his woman back.

He punched the number on his cell phone as he ran back toward town. "Kristos. Where are you?"

"I'm home. What's wrong?"

"Is Lucian with you?"

"Ya."

"Good. I need your help. Fiona's been kidnapped."

Chapter Eleven

WHERE HAD SHE gone wrong? Fiona didn't consider herself a greedy person. She only had a few wishes in life. A successful business, good health, close friends and maybe a man to share it all with.

Well, two out of four wasn't bad. Having a successful business left little time for friends, but Mags and Aunt Bridget were true.

The man to share it all with... Ha!

Fiona sighed and hung her head. She flexed her fingers, attempting to work out the cramp in her hands caused by the bindings strapping her wrists to the arms of the old wooden office chair.

Was it good fortune or a curse to have the man of your dreams be a manipulative alien with superpowers and had enemies who did not hesitate to use you in their plans for retaliation?

Yep, every girl's fantasy.

How many hours had passed since that punk kid she had seen in her shop and two other men burst through her front door? Who were they and what did they want from her?

Besides the obvious. One was not made to don a skimpy silk slip for shits and giggles. The only thing that had stopped Trevor from copping more than a feel while he stripped off her clothing was a reminder from one of the goons that Mr. Smithwick had ordered she be dressed in the clothing of his choosing and presented to him untouched.

Who this Smithwick was, she hadn't a clue, but the Chameleon's name was whispered in the car as they drove her to God only knew where. She had been blindfolded, unable to track where they had traveled, and the office she waited in could have been any old brick-and-mortar building.

The room's furnishings were worn, and appeared mid-twentieth century, but the heavy drapes that covered the windows where she was held were brand new. The interior wall was half plaster and half glass, overseeing the maze of empty desks that comprised the rest of the floor. The layout reminded her of the Daily Planet in the Superman movie.

One man, armed with a rifle, stood guard at the elevator while another blocked the door to the stairway. The goons who took her and Trevor the punk took up space near the worn mahogany desk. Even if she managed to free her hands and make a run for it, that was a lot of muscle to power through. Depending on the next few minutes, it might be a risk worth taking.

"Why so sad, beautiful lady?"

The question brought her focus around and her fingers dug into the arms of the chair.

A shudder that had nothing to do with the drafty room shook her until her teeth chattered. In her relatively young life she had witnessed meanness, bitchiness and an occasional moment of cruelty, but never had she encountered someone who oozed such ruthlessness as the man who glided into the room.

Though he was slight of build and almost frail-looking in stature, he had a snakelike aura that made her stomach pitch with impending doom, and the way the other, much larger, men straightened to attention added to her terror. His suit was impeccable and his strides were just as smooth as the top of his shiny bald head. Malicious amusement sparkled in his dark eyes but otherwise his tan face was a blank slate, which reminded her of the scene from *Silence of the Lambs* when Clarice Starling met Hannibal Lecter for the first time, only Fiona didn't have the protection of prison bars between her and the deadly gentleman circling her chair like a cobra toying with its prey.

He lifted his hand and slowly reached out to trace the curve of her cheek with the tip of his well-manicured finger. The slight pressure against the bruise made her flinch. "Who touched my property?"

Trevor was shoved to the forefront by one of the guards. "Skeeter did, Mr. Smithwick."

"I was just trying to contain her, Mr. Smithwick, sir." Trevor shook and wrung his hands together. "I promise."

"Hmm."

Although the sigh was soft, the contemplative hum evoked the promise of hours of groveling and beatings. Poor schmuck. Fiona winced, partly glad the little shit was going to be reprimanded but at the same time sorry for whatever awaited him in the future. Bet the kid wished he hadn't groped her now.

Smithwick returned his attention to her. "Are you otherwise unharmed?"

"Mentally or physically?" The words croaked out of her dry throat. "Why am I here?"

"You and I have a mutual acquaintance. The Chameleon. I've been wanting to meet with him, but he's rather elusive. You will ensure our introduction." His accent was just as unnerving as his stare. There was a musical lilt that clipped each word at the end like a cleaver hacking through bone. It gave her no indication of his emotions, which had her tensing in preparation for him to strike at the slightest provocation.

"The Chameleon?" She forced a laugh and prayed he'd buy her bluff. "Right. I've seen him a few times, but I don't know him."

His eyes narrowed. "Be careful with what you say, Ms. Corrione. Mr. Skeeter said he saw you together in your shop and at your home. What was the phrase he used? Ah, yes, balls-deep I believe it was."

Heat engulfed her face. Even her earlobes felt as if they were on fire.

It wasn't her actions she was ashamed of, rather the knowledge some pervert had peeped in her windows and leered at her jiggly parts that had bile churning in her stomach. Dear God, how mortifying.

"Oh. Him." She focused on saying every word strong and steady enough to sell the lie. "Well, we were going out, but we broke up. He's a liar and a sleazeball and I never want to see him again."

Well, it wasn't all a lie.

"I see evidence that belies your words, Ms. Corrione." His unnerving finger dipped lower and traced the lacy border of the slip across the slope of her breast then pulled down the cloth to expose a rosy nipple fringed with red nip marks left by Dhavin's teeth. "Unless you've taken another lover so soon."

One of the other kidnappers spoke up. "She has hand-shaped bruises on her ass too, boss. I think she likes it rough."

Fiona pushed against the back of the chair to try to gain some distance from the probing digit. "Stop touching me."

He scooped up her tender flesh in his palm and squeezed the mound tight in his grasp until she cried out. "You do not give me orders. You are mine to do with as I please, when I please." The pressure loosened and he rubbed his hand over the tip as he took a step back. "Make no mistake, I will have you. But not tonight. When I fuck you, you will not bear the mark of another man."

Gee. How encouraging.

Fiona pressed her lips together and fought against the tears making her vision blur. This was ridiculous. Women like her do not find themselves in such incredible situations. Hysteria seized her brain and made her feet bounce with adrenaline as she fought to remain calm and in control.

"Please let me go," she pleaded. "I'm telling you the truth. What the Chameleon and I had was just a fling. He's not going to come for me."

"If he doesn't, I'll still have a use for you. Either way, I win."

"This is crazy. I mean nothing to him. I'm a nobody."

"No, my dear. I believe you are the heart of my greatest enemy. That makes you my most valuable possession."

Dear Lord, if Dhavin has any love for me, please let him find me and get me to safety. Then grant me the strength to kick his ass for dragging me into this mess.

The knock at the office window brought her head up with a startled gasp. At Smithwick's command, the door opened and a guard leaned in far enough to announce, "The jeweler's here."

Smithwick smiled. "Let him in."

Fiona didn't know who to expect to walk through the door with such an innocuous name, but fear closed up her throat and her teeth chattered together. The man who entered the room was dressed in black slacks, Doc Martens and a black cotton long-sleeved shirt. His blond hair was clipped short and the glacial stare made her think the nickname Iceman was better suited. Whoever he was, he was definitely not going to be an ally in helping her escape.

The silver metal briefcase in his beefy hand held her attention like a pregnancy test taken after a one-night stand. Whatever was inside, she did not want to know.

She flinched when the latches clicked open like twin gunfire. Nestled in the foam interior was a strip of metal cases joined together to form a thin belt. The man fitted the strap around her neck like a collar. An electric charge buzzed under her ear and her terror increased tenfold.

A fob passed from the jeweler to Smithwick, who attached the device to a chain he then placed around his neck.

"Do you know what you're wearing?" He smiled and her gaze remained glued to his thumb circling the red button.

Fear held her tongue. She couldn't form a word if a gun were pointed to her head, and she feared that was exactly the case.

"Insurance, my darling," Smithwick answered for her. "If you stray more than one hundred feet from this fob..." He pressed the device and white-hot lightning wrapped around her throat, stealing her vision.

Smoked filled her nostrils and her jaw locked as the excruciating pain burst through her skull. The agony lasted mere seconds, but her teeth continued to ache after the power was disrupted.

Tears poured down her cheeks, wetting the silk covering her chest and soaking the fabric until it was transparent. Fear paralyzed her, making it difficult to do more than wheeze and shake like a tiny mouse before a horrifying lion. Any pretense to maintain the appearance of control was obliterated, gone like light sucked into a black hole.

This scenario was wrong, all horribly wrong. Torture did not exist in her world and her mind was ill equipped to withstand such violence. Maybe if she were a strong, macho solider like Dhavin, she'd be able to spit in Smithwick's eye and dare him to do his worst.

But she wasn't strong, and she wasn't macho.

She was terrified and wanted to go home.

"Ah." The delighted smile in his voice choked her as effectively as the necklace. "I see you understand. Now, now, don't cry. As long as you behave, no harm will come to you. But keep in mind, do not attempt to remove my gift. If you separate the links without this key, the collar will detonate."

Her eyes snapped opened. Detonate?

As if he could read her silent scream he answered, "Yes. Detonate. You may or may not survive the blast, but I can guarantee you won't be as pretty."

Her lips trembled and more tears fell. She felt conscious thought drift away but she found the will to whisper, "Why?"

Smithwick slithered closer and wrapped one of her curls around his finger. "I told you, sweet. To defeat your enemy, you must rip out his heart." His hand moved from her hair to her cheek, his fingertips swirled in the wetness. "Stop these tears. I have a meal prepared for us and I want you to enjoy it. Come."

The bonds around her wrists were released, yet she didn't feel the change in pressure. Fog invaded her body and mind in a dense cushion, leaving her numb to the world and the surreal environment of her new prison. Nothing existed. Not Smithwick. Not the bomb around her neck, nor thoughts of Dhavin to give her comfort or hope. Nothing.

Not even herself.

✦　✦　✦

"YOU ARE SURE you trust these men?" Dhavin asked Brett as they approached one of the city police's safe houses located a mile from the Millstone building. "I'd rather we *Llanos* handle this ourselves."

"Yes, I trust them. And there is no way in hell I'm letting you or anyone, including my husband, walk into another's jurisdiction and take the law into their own hands. Don't think that just because you're family I wouldn't lock your ass behind bars if you don't follow orders."

"This is my fight, Brett. I don't want anyone else to come to harm."

"You're wrong. When it comes to crime, the fight belongs to all of us who wear a badge." She lifted her hand to knock on the door then paused to nail him with a suspicious eye. "You tell me right now if I have to worry about you killing our suspect."

"Smithwick is more than a suspect."

She silenced him with a harsh hiss between her teeth and jabbed her finger in his face. "I will send you back to Cedar right now. Promise me you will not kill anyone."

Dhavin could not, in good conscience, make such a promise. His woman was in danger and the anger and guilt boiling inside him wanted to explode and level the building floor by floor until he had Fiona safe in his arms and Smithwick buried under the rubble. Only his lack of knowledge about the city and his family's interference contained the rage calling him to action.

Deep in the recesses of his mind he knew Brett was right, and he fought to hang on to that thread of sanity. While he'd be justified in killing Smithwick, it wasn't justice. Bale was a prime example of what happened to a man driven by vengeance and the outcome was a sad existence. Fiona needed a man at her side, not in jail. Somehow he was going to have to dig deep and drink from the well of patience. Gods have mercy on those who try to test his restraint.

"Are we leaving?" Brett asked.

He pushed past the lump in his throat to answer. "I can only promise I will try. Fiona's safety is my priority. I will not kill anyone unless we are attacked first. That's the best I can offer."

She nodded then turned to the door and rapped a double beat. "We all want her back safe, D, but we need to do it the right way. Just know we have your back."

The door opened before she finished the sentence.

A man who stood with a smirk on his handsome face waved them into the house. "I was wondering how long you were going to stand there. Are you having second thoughts?"

"Hardly," Brett scoffed and held out her hand. "Thanks for helping, Marco."

"Anything for you, doll." He took her hand and pulled her in for a hug. "You're looking good, Briggs. You're almost pretty. Must be all that mountain air."

While the words were said in jest, the light in his eyes could burn holes in her clothing. The man was lucky Kristos wasn't around, or else he'd need to apply for disability.

Marco's brow furrowed. "What happened to your eyes? I remember them being darker."

"And I remember you having less gray up top. I think your old age is affecting your memory."

"I'm only a year older than you."

"Physically, yes, but I question your mental maturity. Anyway, we can trade barbs later." She touched Dhavin on the arm. "This is the Chameleon and the reason why I called you. Cam, meet Captain Marco DeWinter. I know he'll do all he can to get Fiona back."

Dhavin shook the offered hand. "I'm relying on you, Captain."

DeWinter tightened his grip, his shrewd stare took a calculating perusal of the Chameleon while the pressure of his hand tightened. The captain's strength was rather impressive for someone who was built more like a runner than a fighter. If Dhavin was human, he might have flinched.

After several seconds, the captain released his hold and stepped back. "Interesting uniforms you have there in Cedar,

Briggs. The sword is a nice touch."

"Don't be an ass, Marco."

"Tell me, Chameleon." His lip curled at the name. "Is this your first trip to the city?"

"Yes, it is." At least in this uniform it was.

"Interesting. We had an incident a few months ago involving two men going at each other with swords. They were quite skilled with the weapon. Anyone you know?"

Ah yes, Bale and Kristos. When Bale had been hell-bent on destroying Lucian and Amaryllis, Kristos had confronted the assassin in a very public display of their warrior skills dressed as the Chameleon.

"No. I'm sorry, I'm not familiar with every person in this area who can wield a sword."

The captain didn't look convinced but nodded. "Let me guess." He crossed his arms over his chest. Dhavin did not miss the purposeful flex of his biceps beneath the tight black cotton t-shirt. "You decided to play superhero and messed with someone you shouldn't. Now your girlfriend is paying the price. Man, I wish guys like you would go get real jobs and leave the police work to the professionals."

Dhavin held up a hand to stop the tirade he felt boil up in Brett. "I understand your position, Captain DeWinter. I do all that I can to not interfere in police matters, which I'm certain Sheriff Briggs can attest to. I am the patron of the people, and I always will be. Mr. Smithwick has determined that I am an obstacle on his mission to spread his disease beyond the city, and for that, someone I care about very deeply is now in danger. I ask for your assistance because I want to obey the law, but understand I am more than capable of laying siege and lancing the pus-filled boil that is Smithwick before you've drawn your weapon. Tell me now if we have an accord."

DeWinter drew in a breath and turned to Brett with a raised brow. "Where did you dig up this guy?"

She smiled. "You wouldn't believe me if I told you. What'll it be, Marco? Will you help us or do I let him off his leash? Trust me, it won't be pretty."

He swept them with another long, probing stare then motioned for them to follow him into the dining area where several maps and papers cluttered the surface. A foam board was propped against the wall where more papers and photos were pinned. Two more officers typed on laptops and nodded in greeting as DeWinter gave a hasty introduction.

"After I received your scan of the letter left at the scene, I sent two units to scout the location." DeWinter nudged one of the officers over and began pulling up pictures on the computer. "As you know, the letter S could stand for anyone, and Smithwick is a cool player. No matter what angle we approach from, it's nearly impossible to directly tie him to anything illegal. The Millstone building, and surrounding two blocks, are owned by a company called Sonic Star Development based out of Peru. We believe this company is one of Smithwick's fronts, but again, it's been impossible to confirm.

The whole area is set for demolition next week to make

way for a forty-story high rise condominium, 'cause Lord knows what this city needs is another empty, overpriced, goddamn high-rise."

As he spoke, photos of the building scrolled across the monitor. The slideshow paused at a night-vision picture of two men wearing heavy black winter coats as they slipped into a side door.

"We can't confirm if your girlfriend is in there or not, but we did see a few men who we know are associates of Smithwick's enter the building." DeWinter scrolled to another photo. "This guy is an unknown."

The eyes in the photo glowed with an eerie white light and the face was mostly in shadow, but the long hair and flannel shirt was instantly recognizable.

"Trevor," Brett breathed at the same time Dhavin spat, "Konkle."

DeWinter chuckled. "I take it you all are acquainted."

"Yeah, we're familiar with the little shit," Brett said.

Her words were much more polite than the stream of curses that burst from Dhavin's lips before he caught himself and clenched his jaw together so tightly, everyone in the room flinched at the sound of teeth cracking.

Brett reached out her hand but seemed to think better of it and stepped back. "Cam, what is it?"

When he spoke, his voice was low and rough, as if he swallowed gravel. "He was in her shop. Two days ago I saw him in her shop. He left as soon as I arrived, but he said something to her that upset her. She said it was nothing, just harmless flirting, but she was frightened. Dammit, he was doing recognizance. I should have known she was in danger."

"You didn't know what he was planning." Brett's words were kind but little comfort. "Konkle's small-time. How would we know he's running with big guns like Smithwick? Frankly I'm surprised they let him near their operation at all."

"I should have known. I should have sensed his emotions. This is all my fault."

Anger burned hot, flaying his insides. The pain of his failure bent him in two. His nails bit into his palms, fighting the compulsion to bring the house, and the rest of the block, down around their heads.

"Rein it in, big man." Brett braved his self-inflicted anger and crouched by his side. "We'll get them, and Smithwick and Konkle will be put away forever."

Pull it together. For Fiona, pull it together.

A howl ripped from his throat and the need to destroy took over his limbs. He pulled back his arm and punched down, his fist hammered through to the floorboards and down to the concrete below. The action sated the hunger as well as a Band-Aid on a compound fracture, but it had to do.

As bits of wood and carpet floated in the air, he stood and found three men staring at him with wide eyes and weapons drawn.

He sucked a breath in through his teeth, then another. "What's the plan?"

Thirty minutes later he left the safe house with an earpiece broadcasting back to Brett and DeWinter and a team of SWAT officers circling the neighborhood.

While the police were a necessary presence, he had his own backup following from rooftop to rooftop. External communication was prohibited, so he relied on his empathic ability to track Kristos' and Lucian's movements. As he approached the last block to his target, a shrill whistle caught his attention. A second later a small cylinder landed at his feet.

"What was that?" DeWinter asked through the headset.

"What was what?" Dhavin swept up the canister and kept walking.

"I thought I heard a sound, like a whistle or something."

"Nothing here, Captain. All is quiet. Disturbingly so."

"Well, keep us posted."

"Will do."

Inside the canister was a piece of parchment. The short missive scribbled on the paper did not give him comfort.

Three on one. Five on six. Two on top. No sign of F.

Fiona had to be in that building. She was Smithwick's ace. As long as he had her, Dhavin had to cooperate. Until he had the Chameleon on a leash, he'd have Fiona as close to his side as a tattoo.

Dhavin didn't break stride as he crushed the container and tossed the note down a darkened alley. Since the Chameleon was an expected guest, he didn't bother with stealth. He walked right up the glass rotating door and strode confidently into the foyer, surprising the two men waiting inside with his boldness.

The armed man guarding the elevator stopped him with his gun drawn. "Hold it right there. You can't just waltz right in."

Dhavin smiled and held out his empty hands. "I have a personal invitation. If you could kindly point me in the right direction, I'd greatly appreciate it."

"Fuck you, man. You're not going anywhere until we've searched you."

"Be my guest." He stretched out his arms and waved a greeting toward the brand-new-looking camera he spotted perched above the reception desk.

Rough hands patted down his back and sides before moving up each of his legs.

"Sword." The man with the gun demanded. "And do it slow."

He removed his belt and held out the sword and scabbard, stifling a chuckle when the henchman who took it faltered under the weight and dropped it on his foot.

"Shit, man. That's heavy," he howled and hopped up and down.

"Quit fuckin' off," the gunman slapped the injured man on the back. "Let's go, Hercules."

Two men escorted him into the elevator. As the doors slid shut, Dhavin saw a dark shadow steal across the floor toward the one remaining guard. Soon his sword would be in safe hands.

The elevator stopped on the fifth floor where more men waited by the door. In the middle of the room sat a single table decorated for fine dining, complete with crystal goblets and a floral centerpiece. To the right, a man Dhavin presumed by his expensive suit and smug grin was Smithwick, reclined on a velvet upholstered chair.

Fiona wasn't anywhere to be seen, and a scan with his empathetic powers didn't reveal her presence. Unless she was on the roof with the other two guards, she had to be hidden on one of the other floors. Pray to the Gods Lucian or Kristos located her soon and take her to safety.

"Welcome, Chameleon. My, you are quite the sight to behold, aren't you? I can see how your sheer size alone gave my men pause, but I have to say, I think the headdress is a bit over the top." He lifted a glass filled with champagne. "May I offer you a beverage?"

"I didn't know this was to be a social visit. If you don't mind, I'll get right to the point. You have something of mine. I want it back."

"What a coincidence. You have something of mine as well. Perhaps we can reach an accord."

"What do you want?"

"Peace of mind. I want you to step aside so I may continue my business transactions without interruption."

"If I don't stop you, the police will."

Smithwick chuckled. "Ah yes, the police. They are nothing more than ants at a picnic. Annoying but tolerable. But you, you are a severe thorn in my side. You interfere because you want to, not because it's a job, which tells me you are not swayed by money. Believe me, I wish our paths did not have to cross, but you've left me no choice but to take you out at the knees. Or in this case, the heart."

He pushed the table, wheeling it away from his seat and revealing the object hidden by the table cloth.

Fiona lay on her side, her knees drawn up to her chest. The tiny slip of cloth she wore barely covered her backside and was so sheer, he saw the goose bumps prickling her skin. She stared into the distance, her eyes glassy and unfocused.

Now he understood why her emotional signature was hidden from his powers. Her shock-like condition had sunk deep into her subconscious, rendering her comatose. He might have mistaken her for dead, if not for the shallow rise and fall of her chest.

"What have you done to her?" he shouted and took a step forward only to draw up short at the sound of several rifles cocking as all of Smithwick's men trained their firearms at his torso. He took a breath to calm his franticly beating hearts and strived for his most uninterested tone of voice. "Let her go, Smithwick. Your fight is with me and not this girl. Her only offense is she was available when I had a need. Are you going to kidnap every woman I have intercourse with? You may need a bigger building to house them in."

"A need?" Smithwick chuckled. "Oh, I like how you phrase that. Do you really think I'm stupid? Let's see how much you don't care about her when I do this."

From beneath his jacket he withdrew an amulet that hung around his neck then pressed his thumb to the center. The electric buzz vibrated inside Dhavin's ears, widening his eyes in shock as Fiona jerked and rolled onto her belly with a scream. Her hand went to her throat, her fingers curling around the collar.

"Stop it! Fiona!"

A warning round of bullets sprayed near his feet as he took another step forward. Some of the stray rounds punched holes in the floor near her face.

"Enough," Smithwick shouted as he held up his hand. "I believe our friend understands the point. Relax. It was only a little jolt."

Dhavin's chest bellowed as hard as Fiona's by the time the noise faded. The only benefit to Smithwick's taunt was the death-warmed-over look on her face was gone. The drawback to her regaining consciousness was now her terror flooded his senses, choking him with the bitterness.

"Fiona, love, look at me." Eye contact. That was all he needed. To have her look him in the eye and confirm she knew he was going to get her to safety.

She lifted her head and her eyes were full of fear and a hopelessness he didn't know how to ease. To his horror, she scrambled closer to Smithwick and pressed her face to the side of his leg.

"Obedient as well as beautiful." Smithwick ran his fingers though her tangled curls. "I will enjoy having her by my side. Let me make myself clear, Chameleon. You leave me be and Fiona is treated like a queen. You interfere and she will bear your punishment. Do you understand?"

"Fine. Now let her go." At this point he'd sell his soul to get her out of there. Let the police take care of Smithwick. Once she was safely away, not even an army had the strength to get past his defenses to cause her harm.

"You don't understand. She will stay with me to ensure your compliance. Forever."

Fiona issued a little squeak of distress and rested her hand on Smithwick's thigh as he massaged her scalp. Her red-rimmed eyes pleaded with Dhavin from between the twisted locks.

"SWAT is on the scene, Chameleon." DeWinter's voice came across the earpiece. "Hold steady. We're going to cut the power in two minutes."

Two minutes. His muscles tensed, ready to sweep Fiona into his arms and out the nearest window.

"Do not think I'm playing games with you, Chameleon." Smithwick rubbed his thumb over the fob in light circles. "I see your mind working, planning an avenue of escape for your lady love. If you remove her from my sight, you condemn her to excruciating pain, and I don't need this device to administer it. Believe me, I have her on a short leash."

The flare of fear from Fiona confirmed the threat. She looked back up at him and narrowed her eyes as she drew a deep breath. He felt a steely jolt of determination straighten her spine a second before she turned her head and sank her teeth deep into Smithwick's thigh. As he howled in pain, she reached up and grabbed on to the chain around his neck. At that moment the lights went out, plunging them into darkness.

Dhavin didn't hesitate. He streaked to her side and scooped her up as she screamed in pain. There was a slight lurch as the chain snapped.

"Keep running," she panted against his neck. "I have the button."

Gunfire erupted behind them as the SWAT team stormed out from the stairwells. Dhavin never looked back. He rushed for the gray rectangle of the window and tucked Fiona closer to his chest. Leading with his shoulder, he burst through the glass with her clutching on to his tunic and letting loose another scream. His legs pumped hard in the air as they fell the five stories so when they hit ground he was in motion.

"Captain, I'm on the move," he said. "Racing up Front Street. Fiona's hurt. I need a medic immediately."

"Copy that. Hang a left on 15th. I have aid waiting."

"We're almost there, sweetheart."

Flashing red and blue lights lit up the street corner like a Christmas parade and the sight of the ambulance gave him his first moment of peace in hours.

He laid Fiona on the waiting gurney. "Fiona, still with me?

Help is here. Where are you hurt?"

"No!" She slapped at his hands with more strength than he thought her capable as he reached for the collar. "Don't touch it. It will explode."

"What?" he shouted as the waiting medical personnel all took a step back.

"If you try to take it off without the key, it will explode."

"Where's the key?" He took the chain from her hand. "Is this it?"

"No. This powers the electric shocks. The key's with Smithwick. In his pocket."

"Damn it. Captain, did you hear that? Tell me you have Smithwick in custody."

"Sorry, no sign of him. He disappeared into the tunnels under the building and none of his men are talking, yet. Sit tight. I'll have a bomb tech to you asap."

"Cam! Fiona!" Brett rounded the corner and stopped at his side. "I heard about the bomb. Let me take a quick look."

"Sheriff, I appreciate the offer, but I'd rather leave this to the professionals."

"I'm going to forget you said that. Pay attention to Fiona." She ran her fingers along the collar, lifting and prodding at the device.

Either the cold winter air, the adrenaline racing through her bloodstream, or a combination of the two made her body tremble and the gurney rattled a macabre beat under the death grip she had on the mattress. Her teeth chattered a tarantella and her legs jerked like a marionette controlled by a violent handler. Seeing her struggle brought tears to his eyes, knowing it was he that led her to this misery.

"Why are you standing there?" he bellowed at the medics. "She needs help."

They jumped at his shout and crept toward the stretcher. All of them had their wide-eyed stares trained on the collar.

Brett stepped back. "Relax, guys. The explosives are secure for now. Treat what you can, but wait to administer any IVs until after it's been removed. I don't want any metal or saline anywhere near her until the power in the device is off. Fiona, can you hear me, sweetie? We'll get you out of this. I see the tech coming now."

The tech plodded into Dhavin's view, his gait slow from the weight of the hood and heavy armor covering his entire body down to his thick-soled shoes. Sweat broke out along Dhavin's forehead at the visual reminder of the severity of the situation.

"Howdy, folks," the tech's voice was muffled behind the protective visor. "I need everyone to stand back at least a hundred feet."

Dhavin reached for Fiona's twitching hand and pressed it between both of his. "I'm staying with her."

"Sir—"

"I'm staying!"

The tech's eyes widened. "Okay. Keep her calm and stay out of my way. I don't know what we're dealing with yet and I don't want to rush."

"Fine." He kissed the back of her hand and leaned close to her ear. "Fiona, look at me."

Her eyes squeezed tighter shut and she flinched when the tech covered her in a protective blanket. "I-I can't," she stuttered. "Sorry. I-I'm scared."

"Don't be sorry. Listen to me." He reached under his cowl to remove the earpiece and tossed it into the street. These words were for her alone. "You are so brave. I am in awe of your strength and am so proud of you right now. I'm the one who is sorry. I failed you. You mean so much to me. I never wanted you hurt by my actions."

She remained silent. Only the slight flex of her fingers encouraged him to continue.

"You have no idea how lost I felt when I arrived on this planet. Everything was new and different and lonely. Then I saw you. You were in your shop, helping customers and smiling that beautiful smile of yours. Your aunt said something and you laughed. Your joy reached out to me and enveloped me like a hug. I didn't know how cold I was until I saw you. From that moment on I wanted you for my own, no matter what I had to do to gain your affection. It was selfish of me, and I'm sorry. You have no idea how sorry I am, Fiona."

He pressed another kiss to her hand. "I love you, Fiona. By any name, masked or unmasked, I love you, and I always will."

A tear trickled out from her tightly shut eyelids, but she did not make a sound.

"Shit."

Dhavin looked to the tech. Nothing good ever followed that expletive. "What is it?"

"I nicked a wire."

"What does that mean?"

Fiona's spine arched off the mattress, her jaw clenched tight against a scream.

"The bomb's defused but the power's on. I can't turn it off."

"Get it off her! Get it off!"

"Almost got it." The collar popped open and the tech whipped it out from under her neck.

She collapsed back onto the mattress, her body limp and her chest heaving.

"Fiona." His hands hovered uselessly over her. He didn't know where to touch to offer comfort. "Fiona."

A medic rushed in and attempted to push him aside. "Sir, please move."

"Cam, come on." Brett used two hands and some muscle to pull him far enough away to allow the medic to squeeze in.

"I'm going with her." He sidestepped around her as Fiona was lifted into the ambulance.

"Not yet. DeWinter needs to talk to you. We'll get to the hospital soon. I know you have shadows. They'll follow her."

"No." He ran after the ambulance, pounding on the back door with enough force to shake the hinges loose.

The truck gained speed, and he stuck to its bumper, ignoring the blare of horns and shouts of surprise as he paced the vehicle as it shot down the freeway. A few blocks from the hospital, he was suddenly jerked off his feet by the back of his tunic and carried up the side of a nearby building. His arms and legs flailed in shock as he was tossed onto the rooftop and a giant, booted foot planted its heavy weight on his chest.

"Dhavinllanos, hold your position," Lucian ordered and pressed down harder. Kristos stood with him, dressed in the royal uniform, and the firm set of his lips said he was ready to assist with his restraint if needed.

"I have to see her." He pushed against his cousin's leg.

"I understand, Dhavin, I do, but you can't go in there just yet."

"Fuck off, Lucian. I need to be with her."

"Not like this. You are in uniform and you'll only be in the way. The commotion will cause more harm than good."

"I need her."

"Soon, cousin," said Kristos. "Let them care for her and when she's alone, go to her."

Damn all to the depths of hell! He hated when they were rational.

"Fine. Let me up. They have fifteen minutes. I can't give any more."

Lucian moved his foot, but Dhavin lacked the strength to stand. The events of the day replayed in his mind, making him sicker by the minute. What good was it to have incredible superpowers when they did no good to protect those he loved?

"This is all my fault." He lifted the cowl and wiped at the sweat on his brow. For the first time the royal uniform constricted around his body like shrink-wrap. Suffocating him like a hindrance instead of the honor it was. "If I never was the Chameleon, she'd never have been kidnapped and tortured. What was I thinking? I can't be the Chameleon and be with Fiona. As long as I wear the mask, she'll always been in danger. If not from Smithwick, then someone else."

"We all face that possibility," said Lucian. "We faced it as *Llanos* as well."

"This is different."

Kristos laughed without humor. "No, it's not. The only difference is now you have someone to lose."

"And I almost lost her tonight. I can't ask her to place herself in danger by being with me."

"Then what is the solution?"

He looked down at his chest, his fingers touched the rough scales of the tunic as the protective fabric weighed on his shoulders like never before. The whole of his life centered around protecting the people. Whether he wore the mask or not, his nature was to throw himself into the line of fire and defend those who lacked the strength. It was intrinsic, embedded in his DNA and what made him the *Llanos* warrior he was. Despite any good intentions he may have to let others run into danger first, he doubted he could stand on the sidelines. For as long as he lived, he'd do whatever it took to offer his protection.

In this case the one who needed protecting was Fiona.

"There is only one solution." His breath caught as he truly understood the choice he had to make. "I'm going to have to end things with Fiona."

Chapter Twelve

FIONA KEPT HER gaze on the slice of pie before her and swirled the tines of her fork in the velvety concoction as her stomach revolted at the thought of taking another bite.

Betty Sue's chocolate cream pie was the only recipe Fiona conceded was better than hers, but even the sinfully rich goodness was tasteless on her tongue. Perhaps it was due to the fact her taste buds had yet to recover from the electric shocks she took to the head.

Or…maybe it was because every person in the café watched her from the corner of their eye and whispered behind cupped hands.

News of her kidnapping and relationship to the Chameleon had been the hot topic around town during the two days she spent in the hospital. According to Aunt Bridget, business was booming at the shop with people wanting to ask her questions and hoping to see the masked superhero.

Good luck with that. The man professed his love at her sickbed then disappeared without a trace. No note. No coded message. Nothing. If not for the fact that every terrifying minute from the moment she bit into Smithwick's leg to when the bomb tech set off the collar was burned into her memory, she might have chalked up the pretty speech as a delusion.

And if he did suddenly appear before her, what the hell would she say? Thanks for saving me? You're an ass for placing me in danger? You love me, great?

God, perhaps it was for the best that she had this time to attempt to sort out her feelings. At this point she was just as likely to jump into his arms as she was to run screaming in the other direction.

"Fiona."

She started and looked over at the sheriff as her cheeks burned hot with embarrassment at being caught not listening. "Sorry, Sheriff. I didn't mean to zone out there."

"Please, call me Brett." She smiled and took a sip of her coffee. "Actually, I think I'd be concerned if you didn't have a million thoughts running through your head right now. You've had a lot to deal with lately."

"Yeah, I guess you have been in my shoes. Sort of."

"That I have, but I didn't invite you out to put you on display. If all the stares are making you uncomfortable, we can leave and talk elsewhere."

"No." She straightened in her seat and squared her shoulders. A few stares were not going to prevent her from living a normal life. "I'm fine."

Before the Chameleon entered her world, it was not unusual to see her sitting in the diner and enjoying a slice of pie. There was no reason for her not to indulge in a treat with him gone. May this small scoop of deliciousness be the first in the road back to normalcy.

"Good." Brett licked the last of the cream from her fork and placed it on the table. "Fiona, I want you to know that I'm here to answer any questions you may have. You and I are members of a very secret club. For a while I was the only member, and I wished I had someone to talk to. Loving a *Llanos* isn't easy, and believe me, I fought it every step of the way, but the reward…man, totally worth the leap. Most days." She winked. "From what I've seen is that when a *Llano*s loves, it's with their entire being. I think it's in their genetic wiring, but whatever it is, I'm grateful every day I have Kristos in my life."

"But Kristos isn't…him." She gave a quick glance around. Who knew who was eavesdropping.

"True. True. But I do know that while he didn't have the best of plans, he did have the best of intentions. Now I can't promise he won't do stupid shit in the future, but I can promise the make-up sex is amazing."

Fiona laughed and her cheeks heated further. "That's nice things worked out for you and Kristos, but we're different. How do I know if I fell in love with the man or the mask?"

"What does your heart tell you?"

That at times coincidence was a wicked bitch.

Or was it coincidence that at that precise moment the door to the diner opened and the Kilsgaard clan entered. The sight of all that masculinity sucked the oxygen from Fiona's lungs.

Lordy, but they were a handsome group of fellas and she wasn't the only one staring as they took their seats in a booth across the room.

Since he wasn't on duty, Dhavin was dressed in jeans and a formfitting Henley t-shirt that somehow made his muscles appear larger than she remembered. He looked so rugged and manly, and she realized this was the first time she had seen him not in a uniform. Well, besides being naked, of course. She didn't even know he owned a pair of jeans. How insane was that? Beside the bedroom and her shop, they had spent practically zero time together in a setting that included a touch of reality. How could she be in love with someone she knew so little about?

But she was. Heaven help her, she loved him to the point of physical pain.

Yes, he lied about his secret identity. Compared to the malice she recently experienced, he was forgiven for the hurt to her pride. Yet it was her time with Smithwick that hammered home the dangers he faced daily with not one, but two jobs he took obvious pride in. If the stories she heard about his home planet were true, being a *Llanos* warrior was more than a job but a birthright passed from generation to generation because of the honor and strength passed through genetic code. Dhavin's happiness stemmed from his ability to protect. To ask him to stop would be pure selfishness on her part.

She sneaked another glance in his direction. Though he had a menu in his hands, he watched her from beneath his lashes. The furrow in his brow silently asked about her well-being and she swore she felt his concern as if she were the one with empathic powers.

If this had been a movie, there'd be millions of women screaming at the screens for her to run to him. Hell, she'd be one of them. But the burns around her neck kept her butt in her seat and the taste of her own cowardice burned her tongue.

She buried her face in her hands and choked back a sob. "I have no idea what to do."

"Why don't you ask him?"

"I can't. He's part of the problem."

Brett tapped her on the arm. "Not him. *Him.*"

Fiona looked up and in the direction Brett pointed. Her jaw dropped and the noise in the café faded away as one by one the other diners turned toward the big picture window.

The Chameleon stood on the other side of the glass. Tall and imposing with a jaw as hard as granite. Light from the café played with the scales of his tunic, reflecting the stunned faces of the patrons. When she met his gaze, he beckoned her to come out with a crooked finger. Her head whipped back to the booth where Dhavin sat with his two cousins. He nodded an encouragement for her to go.

"What are you waiting for?" Brett asked with a knowing smile. "Go."

"I don't understand." Who the hell was this guy?

Brett waved at her in a shooing motion. "Just go."

Jell-O invaded her trembling legs as she slid over the bench seat and walked with halting steps across the room. A cold breeze slapped her windbreaker against her body when she opened the door and the shivers grew when he motioned with his head and crossed the street to the park where he waited for her under the bright streetlight.

As she drew closer, she noticed this man was taller than Dhavin, but much leaner. The uniform still stretched over his shoulders, but the pants didn't cling to his thighs in the same way they hugged Dhavin's and his waist was much smaller in circumference. She almost wanted to run back inside and get him a sandwich. Tragic was the word that stabbed her in the heart as he peered at her with eyes so dark, she wondered if their black color was natural or a byproduct of his internal pain. If she were to ever see him again without the mask, she was certain she'd be able to recognize him. Such melancholy was unforgettable.

"Who are you?"

"Play along," he murmured, barely moving his lips.

He looked over her shoulder and her gaze followed. All of the diners from the café were pressed against the windows and some spilled onto the sidewalk. Even some of the customers of the nearby stores had joined the gathering crowd.

The rolling of her stomach grew into a tsunami-sized tidal wave. What fresh hell had she stepped into? Thank goodness she hadn't eaten a lot of that pie.

"Fiona, I was hoping to see you tonight," the Chameleon said in a booming voice certain to travel all over the neighborhood. He glanced down at his hand and she saw writing scribbled across his big palm. "I can no longer be romantically involved with you."

"What?"

"Now, now, do not cry. Your tears will not move me," he continued in a stilted cadence. "I know you have another in your lite. Life? Oh, fuck me. Look…" His posture relaxed but the intensity in his expression remained fierce as he spoke low and for her ears only. "There is a price that comes with wearing this uniform, and I've paid it. As long as I'm in your life, you'll always be in danger. It will be best for everyone if the Chameleon retains his solitary existence."

His gaze shifted to over her head, and when she looked back, she spotted Dhavin in the gawking crowd. The tension in his stance made him appear like a statue amongst the locals who jostled for a better view. One hand covered his mouth while his free arm banded across his chest as if to hold himself back from interfering.

"He loves you," the Chameleon said with a wistfulness that brought tears to her eyes. "And you're terrified."

"I am not."

"Liar. I sense you. Here." He touched his chest. "Believe me, I don't blame you. To entrust all that you are to another takes a courage I don't think I'll ever possess. In fact, I think it's blessed only upon the insane. But he does love you. That's why he's willing to give up the mask. If you were harmed again because someone wanted to lash out at him, he would never recover."

"But I can't ask him to give it up."

"You don't have to. He does it willingly. Look, woman, I'm the last person to give advice on relationships, but I am an expert on regret. The next step you take is your choice. Do not base your decision on fear."

"I think that's easier said than done."

"And I think you're stronger than you believe. So, what say you?"

Butterflies beat a frenzy in her stomach as she clenched her teeth and took a deep breath through her nose. The Chameleon had said the one word that made all her doubts fall into place. Regret.

What was that saying? You can try and succeed, or you can do nothing and fail for certain. Relationships were about give and take, and if what this man said was true, then Dhavin had given up a huge part of himself for her. The least she could do was try.

Fiona lifted her chin and shouted, "You know what? I don't need all this drama. You're more flash than substance anyway. If you want to break up, fine, so be it. I never want to see you again."

The corner of his mouth lifted into a tiny grin. "Goodbye, Fiona. It was fun while it lasted." He turned to leave then stopped short. When he turned back to face her there was a light in his eyes that sent a tingle down her neck. "Before I go, here's a little something to remember me by."

In two steps, she was in his arms, his lips pressed to hers. After the flare of surprise faded, she realized the kiss was actually quite pleasant. Was it a perquisite that all who wore the tunic be a good kisser?

She swayed on her feet when he stepped away. The smile on his lips softened the carved lines around his mouth.

"Good luck, little human."

One second he was standing before her, the next, he was a streak across the square, scaling the side of city hall before disappearing into the light of the moon.

Holy cow, he had powers too.

With the Chameleon gone, Fiona felt the weight of over forty expectant stares boring into her back. A peek over her shoulder confirmed that some of the biggest gossips in town just witnessed her breaking up with a legend. How is one supposed to react?

Brett waved in her direction and pointed to her cheek with a frown. Fiona caught the hint and began to cry, scrunching her face tight to hide her dry eyes. The only man she ever cried over was Dhavin, she didn't have any experience in this situation.

"Fiona, it will be okay." Brett jogged to her side and patted her on the back. With a comforting arm across Fiona's shoulder, she led her back across the street. "Guys like the Chameleon can't commit. They're adrenaline junkies."

Several of the diners nodded their agreement.

"Okay, people, break it up. Nothing to see here," the sheriff shouted. "Dhavin, why don't you see Fiona home? She doesn't need all of us gawking at her humiliation."

"I'd be happy to." He held out his hand. "May I escort you home, Fiona?"

She stared at his outstretched palm, knowing there was more to the simple request. Ah, now this was the big test. Did she have the courage to take his hand and take a step toward the future?

Dhavin's hand trembled the longer she stared. That little tell gave her the strength to take his hand. The warm press of his fingers and the huge sigh he released made real tears cling to her lashes.

He held tight to her hand as they walked in silence down the street to where her car was parked behind her shop. She reached out to open the door, but he stopped her with a soft grunt. His hand shook with a fine tremor as he fingered the scarf around her neck. "May I?"

She nodded and allowed him to untie the fabric. Once removed, he laid his fingers against the burn marks. "Fiona—"

The pain that cracked his voice broke her heart. "Shh. I know. I know, Dhavin."

His hand traveled up to sweep along her jaw then turned to brush the backs of his fingers over her cheek. Once he began, it was as if he couldn't stop touching her. From her face down to her hips, his hands told her all the things she saw shining in his eyes, but were trapped behind the tight press of his quivering lips.

As if she was able to communicate any better. Where was she to begin? There was so much to say, so much to discuss. What if she chose the wrong words?

Words. Huh. No, in this case words weren't enough.

She brushed his hands away from her face and leaned in for a kiss. His arms were around her, pulling her against the warm haven of his body as he slanted his mouth over hers.

Connection. Passion. Need. The rush of blood in her ears. The clutch of his hands on her hips. Fiona wanted Dhavin. Dhavin wanted Fiona. Only action was suitable enough to convey that desire.

When her lungs began to burn she pulled back enough to gasp for breath.

He touched his forehead to hers. "Does this mean I'm for-given?"

"Yes. Just…don't lie to me again."

He smiled, deepening the dimple near his mouth. "I prom-ise. I love you, Fiona."

"I love you too. Are you really planning on not being the Chameleon anymore? Please don't stop because of me."

"I don't want to quit, but I definitely need to take a hiatus. There's this girl I'm trying to convince to be mine forever. It will take time to woo her properly."

"How much time?"

"As long as she needs."

"Would a sleepover tonight be a good start?"

The joy shining in his eyes lowered to a sinful simmer.

"Sounds perfect, but I plan on spending a lot more time, if needed."

"Good." She trailed a line of kisses along his jaw. "Who was that man anyway?"

"The last of our kinsmen here on Earth, and until a few minutes ago a friend. That kiss was not part of the plan." He nipped at her bottom lip. "And you didn't need to enjoy it so much."

"I just needed to make sure I was making the right choice. And I did." She took the keys from her pocket and held them out. "You want to drive?"

"I don't know how."

"How to what?"

"Drive."

A dull throb took residence between her eyes as her brain tried to comprehend his words. "Are you kidding? How is that possible? What about for work?"

His shoulders lifted and fell as if he hadn't dropped a major bombshell. "I walk or ride as the passenger. You forget I haven't been here very long. I haven't learned yet."

"How did I not know this about you?"

Here it goes again. Just when she was ready to take a leap of faith, something reached out and strapped her feet back to earth.

The pain in her head began to circle, forming a dizzying cyclone of panic as she questioned her sanity about loving someone she knew next to nothing about.

"Fiona. Fiona. Breathe." He cupped her face. "Would you love me more if I knew how to drive?"

"I—" Well, when he put it that way… Heat seared her checks. "I may need a lot of time."

"As long as it takes." He kissed the tip of her nose. "You're worth it, Fiona."

The depth of his confidence scared the crap out of her, but also gave her the much needed push to believe in her strength. And his. Dhavin's love gave her the wings to fly into the unknown. To soar on the current of possibility and have faith he would be there to catch her when she stumbled.

"Take me home. Tonight, I want to make love to *you*, Dhavin."

He closed his eyes on a groan. "Your wish is mine, *konkattie*."

"Are you ever going to tell me what that means?"

The promise in his chuckle sent a delicious shiver down her back. "Not yet. That's one secret I want to keep to myself for a while."

"Careful, Kilsgaard. I have a razor and know how to use it."

His laughter echoed down the alley. "I'm counting on it, *konkattie*."

Epilogue

SOFT LANTERN LIGHT and the colorful splash of spring flowers greeted Fiona as she opened the door to the Anderson's cottage. Dhavin had been in charge of the decorations, and her man had done an excellent job.

The king-sized mattress on the floor covered in satin made her laugh. "No futon? Where's the bedframe?"

"There is a good possibility of furniture being destroyed. I thought it best to remove them."

The unspoken promise in his words had her thighs quivering. The night's events were about more than a romantic evening spent together. This was like a wedding night on steroids and the expectations of what was to come caused a whirlpool to churn in her belly.

Dhavin wrapped his arm around her waist and nuzzled the area under her ear. "Why are you so nervous? Having second thoughts?"

Lying about her emotions was never an option with him, so she didn't bother to try. "Sort of. I want this to be perfect."

"You're with me, so it already is."

"Will this hurt?"

"I don't know. I've never done it before, but I don't think so." He spun her to face him, his hands rubbed up and down her arms. "Ready?"

The certainty in his eyes drove all hesitation from her mind. "Yes." She bussed his cheek with her lips. "Give me one minute to set up dessert."

From her bag she withdrew a fondue pot and a Sterno can. "Why don't you get more comfortable?" She glanced at him from over her shoulder and laughed when she saw he had already stripped down to his boxer-briefs and was laid out on the mattress with his hands behind his head and his pectorals pulsing.

Talk about a feast for the eyes. Dhavin was all dips and valleys of golden skin that had her salivating for a taste. And that smile. Dazzling white and welcoming. He was perfect and all hers.

Here was a man who loved her, faults and all. She laughed again, filled to bursting with so much unadulterated joy, she swore she was high from the rush.

"Ah, Fiona." He put his hand on the center of his chest. If she had been from his planet, she'd know exactly how he felt, but since she couldn't sense his emotions, he never hesitated in telling her how much she meant to him. "You bring me to my knees with one look."

"I plan on doing more than just look. Let me finish. Don't move." Admiring him from the corner of her eye, she went back to her task.

"Hurry." His hand trailed down his body and disappeared under the waistband of his briefs.

"Believe me, I am."

It took three tries for the flame to ignite and a nice little blaze heated the pot of caramel sauce. She set the pot on the floor near the mattress then kicked off her shoes and peeled away her socks.

"Undress slowly," he requested, firmly stroking his cock at a languid pace.

She felt her smile stretch to match his anticipatory grin. Thumbing the button of her jeans open, she slid them down her legs with an extra shimmy for good measure. Her blouse was next to float to the floor, followed by her lacy bra. She cupped the heavy weight of her breasts in each hand and pinched her puckered nipples.

"*Jesu*," he groaned and sat up on his knees. "You are so sexy. Go faster."

"Hurry. Slow down. Go faster. Which one is it?"

"Both." He pulled her down onto the mattress and smoothed his warm hands over her body from neck to thigh. With a firm tug, her panties were ripped and tossed aside.

"Do you always have to tear my clothes?" she murmured against his neck as she traced his pulse with her tongue. "The pretty ones are expensive."

"If you don't wear any at all, then it's not an issue."

She laughed again and pushed against his chest, encouraging him to lie down. "I'm hungry and you're my treat."

"Yes ma'am." He raised his hands over his head. "Would you like to restrain me?"

"Do I have to?"

"No, I promise to behave."

"You'd better. Brett lent me the molybendite chain that drains your powers. I'm not afraid to use it."

"You'd use it too, you little witch. Trust me, you'll want me at my full strength when I slide inside you."

He was right, but he didn't need to know that now.

She hooked her thumbs into the waistband of his shorts and pulled them down his legs, biting back a moan when his pulsating cock sprang free and rested on his belly. The head was purple and his bare sac was already drawn tight against his body.

She pressed a kiss to his balls. "For me?"

"For us. Don't stop. That feels fantastic."

"Just wait, baby." She reached for the basting brush she had laid near the pot then ran the two-inch-wide tip up the inside of his thigh.

His legs twitched and his panting grew louder as she continued to make swirly patterns along his erection. When a drop of pre-cum pooled in the slit, she removed the brush and dipped it into the warm caramel. She straddled his waist and painted a line down the center of his torso then followed the path with the flat of her tongue.

With the edge of the brush she traced the double-ring tattoo encircling his arm that signified his status as a royal guard of Skandavia.

"Do you miss your home?" she asked.

"You're my home, Fiona." He stroked her cheek with the tips of his fingers. "If I was forced to choose between going back and you? No question, with you is where I always want to be."

The conviction in his voice brought tears to her eyes, which she hid by returning to her work. Over his nipples and down his sides she painted his skin then licked him clean, making sure to capture every drop of sugar.

When his pleading became an unending chant, she brushed a healthy dollop of caramel down the length of his straining cock. Once he was completely painted, she licked an area wide enough for her fingers to encircle the base, then attacked him with her tongue. As she sucked him into her mouth, the heady taste of his pre-cum mixed with hot sugar pooled in her mouth. Her cheeks hollowed as she swallowed, making his hips jerk and pressing his cock deeper down her throat.

His speared his fingers into her hair. "Fiona. Stop. Wait, no. Don't stop. Arg. Stop. I'm going to come, but I want to come in your pussy." With a growl, he pulled her off and was across the room before she could draw a breath.

His chest bellowed and a red slash graced each cheek as he stared at her with wild eyes. He reached for his cock and squeezed the base hard, drawing in deep breaths.

"Lie back," he commanded in a voice do deep, she felt the

vibration in her clit.

Once she had reclined, he stalked back to the mattress and knelt between her spread legs. He picked up the brush and tossed it into the air, catching it by the handle. "My turn."

Oh. My. God.

With one hand he cupped her breasts together and painted a wide swath of caramel across both nipples in a single stroke. A circle was drawn around her navel followed by a line across each hipbone. The roughness of his tongue alternated by the smoothness of the brush made her head swim and her limbs feel like molten chocolate oozed in her veins. By the time he pushed her thighs farther apart she was ready to scream.

"You are so wet." The awe in his voice was like an electric jolt to her libido.

He swirled the bristles around her clit and down the folds of her sex before latching on to the bud with his mouth. His moans vibrated along her skin, extracting more of her cream. "Caramel and Fiona. My new favorite flavor."

As he supped from the cup between her thighs, Fiona grabbed handfuls of sheet, her sticky fingers adhered to the bits of fabric he had shredded when she had gone down on him. She writhed in his grip, floating on currents of heat. He slid two fingers into her sheath, triggering an orgasm that swept over her like an unseen tidal wave and dragged her deeper into the vortex of pleasure. Dhavin was the only man she knew who could take her from zero to sixty in a heartbeat and leave her aching for more.

Tremors continued to shake through her and her pussy spasmed as he notched the bare blunt head of his cock at the entrance of her channel and pushed, invading her slowly until his smooth sac rested against her ass. The feel of her velvet walls rippling along his hot length was too exquisite. Dhavin's eyes rolled back and his lips pulled tight over his teeth as her hips rolled, seeking more of the sweet torture.

"Still your hips," he panted. "I don't want to come yet."

"I can't." She bucked and locked her legs around his waist to pull him in deeper. "It's too good."

"Damn it, woman." He pinned her to the mattress with his body. "I don't want this to be over before I've begun."

She laughed. "We can do this again." She kissed his lips. "And again." Another kiss. "And again."

He sank into her, thrusting his tongue into her mouth in time with his hips, and she rejoiced at this break in his control. The heavy press of his body, the frantic lunges as his cock stretched her sheath in a delicious burn, she loved it all. Sweat broke out on their skin, allowing her hands to slip and slide, reveling in the flex of his muscles under her palms.

Suddenly he reared up, shifting so his knees were on the floor and pulled her down so her ass hung off the mattress. At this angle his cock speared deeper, rubbing the sweet spot in her cunt with each thrust.

His hands cupped her breasts. "Fiona. Fiona, look at me."

To open her eyes felt as if she had to swim to the surface in a pool of warm pudding, the rich thickness of impending orgasm was too addictive to concentrate on anything else.

"Fiona. En la nire de demos, Y tesktsen a mi band brigde."

She was clueless as to what he was saying, but the intent was unmistakable. Her lungs grew tight and she swore her heart beat out of her chest and rested in his palm as his fingers kneaded her breasts. The language he spoke was so melodic, tears fell from her eyes at the beauty of it, an internal flame ignited in her belly and sparkly lights floated in her vision.

His hips pumped harder and his voice grew more guttural. The only word she recognized was her name spoken on a growl as sweat dripped from his forehead. A white light replaced the brown of his eyes as ripples of rapture speared to her womb.

"Dhavin," she cried, her body twisting, gripped by the intense pleasure.

"Fiona, in the name of the Gods, I claim you as my bonded mate." His voice was so low, she felt the rumble in his words more than heard them. "In my hands I hold your life and your love. Two precious gifts I ask you to entrust in my care. In return, I promise to be all things you need. Say you accept me. Say you accept my gift and bond as one for eternity."

As if she could resist.

The fire in her belly erupted as she screamed, "Yes. Yes. Yes."

Dhavin's shouts joined hers. The sound went into her ears and poured down her spine like champagne, sweet and bubbly. Everything he felt, she experienced as well. From the viselike grip of her sheath around his cock to the bolt of electricity that raced up his shaft as his cum splashed her cervix.

With each ragged breath she drifted back into her body and the connection to Dhavin lessened. Somewhere in the distance a creature howled a garbled cry. Was the sound growing closer?

Dear Lord, that was her trapped under the massive weight of a sated man.

With her face smashed against his chest, she lacked the energy to do anything more than sink her teeth into his pectoral to get him to move.

He yelped and rolled to his side, tucking her against him. His hands swept up and down her back, caressing over her hips as her skin cooled.

"Is that it?" she croaked out between sniffles. "Are we bonded?"

"You have to ask?" He laughed and his voice sounded just as damaged.

"I just want to make sure there wasn't more. If there is, I think I may die."

He kissed her forehead. "Death by orgasm. What a way to go."

"Your eyes, they were glowing—" She gasped as she looked up at him. "Hey. A second ago they were white, now they're brown again."

Only now the color was different. Gone were the gold flecks that used to sparkle when he teased her and instead a touch of green deepened the color.

"Look." His lifted a lock of her hair that had darkened to match his nearly black locks. "The mark of the bond. We're connected now."

"Earlier, I felt everything you did. You're right. I am soft all over."

Her head bounced against his chest as he laughed. "That's one of the many things I love about you. You're wonderful. Inside and out."

She settled deeper into his hold and enjoyed the stroking of his palms over her curves. The incessant blare of his cell phone broke her reverie.

"Who do we get to murder?" she asked without opening her eyes.

He groaned as he stretched his arm as far as he could reach, barely able to latch a finger around the handle of their overnight bag to drag it close enough to retrieve the offending instrument.

"That was Amaryllis. She left a text congratulating us on our bonding."

"How did she know? I didn't tell a soul."

"When she bonded with Lucian, the entire city felt their connection. I guess she felt ours."

"All the way out to the city? That's crazy. Will that happen every time we make love now?"

"I don't think so. But I'm not going to let that stop me if it did."

The phone blared again and the tension that strung him tight when he looked at the display was enough to bring her head up in concern.

"Who is it now?"

He wiped his hand over his mouth and across his chin. "The Chameleon's needed. Kristos and Brett are at a childbirth class, otherwise he'd go."

She rolled off his chest and pushed at him with her hands and feet. "Bring me a blanket and lock the door on your way out."

"I can't leave you on our bonding night."

"I knew what I was in for when I agreed to be with you. Will you be back tonight?"

"I won't let anything stop me."

She took his hand and pressed a kiss to his palm. Inside she was glad for a moment alone to sleep and recharge for another round. "I'll be right here when you're done. Be safe."

Her eyes drifted shut before she finished her sentence. His hot breath bathed her cheek as he kissed her and whispered in her ear, "Sleep, my love. When I return, I'm not letting you out of my sight for at least a week."

"I'm counting on it, my little sex kitten." She smiled.

About Anna Alexander

Anna Alexander is the award winning author of the Heroes of Saturn and the Sprawling A Ranch series. With Hugh Jackman's abs and Christopher Reeve's blue eyes as inspiration, she loves spinning tales of superheroes finding love. Anna also loves to give back and has served on the board for the Greater Seattle Romance Writers of America as chapter president and on the committee for the Emerald City Writers Conference.

Sign up to receive news about Anna's latest releases at http://eepurl.com/Q0tsz

Website

annaalexander.net

Facebook

facebook.com/pages/Anna-Alexander/282170065189471

Twitter

twitter.com/AnnaWriter

Newsletter

http://eepurl.com/Q0tsz

Also by Anna Alexander

Heroes of Saturn Series

Hero Revealed

Hero Unleashed

Hero Unmasked

Hero Rising

Men of the Sprawling A Ranch Series

The Cowboy Way

The Marlboro Man

To Have Faith

Elite Metal

Bound by Steele

Adamantium's Roar

Elite Ghosts

Thallium's Submission